Amish Made

Marisa Meyer

Published by Trellis Publishing, 2021.

This is a work of fiction. Similarities to real people, places, or events are entirely coincidental.

AMISH MADE

First edition. July 9, 2021.

Copyright © 2021 Marisa Meyer.

ISBN: 979-8224115228

Written by Marisa Meyer.

AMISH MADE

MARISA MAYER

AMISH MADE

Chapter 1

The sun was still hidden behind the hills of Herzberger Creek, and the cold chill of the morning air cut through Faith's coat penetrating her bones, but despite the frosty bite, she had work to do. She trod along the muddy path that lead to the barn, bucket in one hand and basket in the other. While her grandmother and her younger sister tended to breakfast and the laundry she would tend to milk the cows and collect the eggs from the chicken coop for the market.

Although no-one dared to say it out loud, everyone thought it—Faith should find a husband, Faith shouldn't be running a farm on her own, Faith shouldn't do this and that. They may all greet her with utmost politeness, but their whispers never went unnoticed. But who were they to preside over her life and what she was capable of.

She was only twelve and her sister barely six when her father died. It was a senseless crime that took his life and the perpetrator was never found, not because he evaded the law, but because the church refused to involve the law. The act so cruel and unkind had left her mother in despair, to a point where she was no longer capable of caring for them. Was it not for her *grossmammi*, who eventually had to come and help run the household and teach her and her sister what to do, they would never have survived. Two years after her father's death, her mother died, supposedly of a broken heart—and it was there and then that Faith had decided, her heart was hers for the keeping. Now years later, with her *grossmammi* much older than and not as agile as she was in her youth, she had to run the farm and manage the market in order to keep afloat. Becky, her younger sister would also soon be married to Caleb, and she wanted it to be a special occasion.

Faith pulled the stool closer and placed the bucket under the cow's udders, with her head planted against the side of the animal she watched the milk rise. No sooner had she started when the chickens clucked and crowed frantically from the coop just outside the barn.

"Oh heavens!" she cried out, "The foxes!"

She shoved the stool back, sending it rolling across the floor, grabbed the rake and rushed outside.

"Shoo! Shoo!" she called out, poking at the fox that dug his way into the coop. "Go, get!! Becky!"

The fox had one of the hen's locked in his jaw and was not planning on letting go of his catch either.

"Becky!" she called again, but the house was too far from the barn for her sister to hear.

She reached for the door to the coop and flicked the latch for it to swing open. Almost desperately she ducked into the coop, feathers and straw flying everywhere. The fox darted left and right and then froze. His black beady eyes locked on her and the limp body of the bird hanging from its mouth.

"It's no use, let him go or he might turn his attack on you."

It was a man's voice who spoke behind her as she stood challenging the fox, that slight distraction when she turned to see who it was, was all the fox needed. In a brown flash it darted between her legs and ran out of the coop, disappearing across the field into the tree line that bordered the farm.

"I had him, and you had to go and distract me," she muttered, plucking feathers and straw from her hair.

He stepped forward and held out his hand as she ducked to exit the coop but she ignored his gesture and dusted herself off.

"I'm sorry, I heard someone screaming, and I came to investigate," he apologized tucking his hands in his pockets.

The man had the kind of voice and face that would stop anyone in their tracks, even someone like Faith, who wouldn't dare to daydream about love and commitment to marriage. But here he was, and an Englischer of all things. He was tall, with stylish black hair. He wore a brown leather jacket that made him look strong and muscular with a checked blue shirt, faded jeans and cowboy boots with steel tips.

"I was calling my sister."

"And what would your sister have done?"

Faith blinked and tucked her hair back under her cap. What exactly would Becky have done why did she call her in the first place? Then she realized.

"Oh no, the milk!" she cried out, spun around and ran to the barn.

The milk was all over the floor. She had been in such a rush to save the chickens, she hadn't thought of putting the milk aside before she ran out and now she would never have enough for the cream she ought to sell at the market.

"Is there anything I can help with?"

"No," she blurted out. "There's nothing you can do. You need to leave."

"But maybe I can..."

She spun around and looked at him, on the verge of snapping at him, but she reminded herself to treat all people like God would treat them.

"Please sir, I appreciate you trying to help, but there is really nothing left to do. Now if you'll excuse me."

She didn't bother to find out his name, or figure out what he was doing here on the farm. She had no desire for small talk or anything. Her day had irrevocably been ruined. Now the only thing left for her to do, was to bake scones and flat breads, and take what was left of the vegetables to the market.

Chapter 2

"John, is that you?"

"Yes Aunt Mae, it's me," he said as he entered the kitchen and planted a kiss on his aunt's cheek. "Did you sleep well?"

"Oh you know how it goes, when you get old, your body seems to have a mind of its own, all night long my legs felt as if they wanted to be detached from the rest of me."

John arrived a few days ago, merely to settle the sale of his aunt's farm and help her move in with her neighbour and friend where she could finally settle down and have the help she needed. But this place reminded him too much of his childhood. Outsiders to the Amish community, his parents often brought him along to visit his aunt. And as a child only wanting to make new friends, he was never allowed to go out and meet the other young kids. They don't allow English kids to play with them, his father always said. So every fall when they visited, he had to sit all by himself and read book after book, or play with his imaginary friends. He had hated coming here as a child.

"Where did you run off to earlier?" his aunt asked, interrupting his train of thought.

He sat down and reached for the muesli. "Oh I heard a woman call for help so I went to investigate."

"Oh goodness, was it serious?"

He chuckled, "Not as serious as it sounded. A fox caught one of her chickens."

"Oh, that must have been Faith. Poor child, it's a crying shame she has to run that entire household all by herself."

John's brows shot up, "That was Faith?"

"Yes, you do remember her, don't you John?"

He sure did. But all he could remember of her was the freckle-faced teenager who refused to give him a second glance or even say hello. And earlier when she spun around to look or rather glare at him, he had to keep himself from reacting at the sight of her beauty. She had the bluest eyes, with rosy cheeks colouring her porcelain skin. If he could have pinched himself there and then he would have. Not once did he even consider her to be Faith Bontrager.

"It was her father who was murdered, wasn't it?"

His aunt sighed softly, "Yes it was, poor thing, and two years later her mother died of a broken heart."

John frowned and scooped a spoon full of yogurt and muesli and shoved it into his mouth. Back when this all went down the entire community had been thrown into disarray. The local Amish people all blamed the Englischers for luring criminals onto their lands with all their fancy cars and worldly belongings. And the English farmers all stood their ground and blamed the Amish for being so stubborn and for not allowing the law to do their work. John, together with his parents had been down to visit his aunt at the time, and he remembered clearly how the young Amish kids used to throw rocks at them passing by. It took a few meetings between the Amish council and a few English farmers to come to an agreement and settle matters diplomatically. The Amish would benefit from the security the Englischers offered, and the Englischers would benefit from supporting the farmer's market.

"So she's running the farm all on her own then?"

His aunt sipped her tea and waved her hand dismissively. "That one will never settle. She's far too caught up in doing a man's work than being bothered with raising a family of her own. The Amish don't fancy a woman with such willpower."

He smirked and thought; at least she was standing up for herself. "It's good to know nothing much has changed on the Amish front then."

His aunt laughed and placed her cup on the table. "She's actually a lovely girl, but she's untouchable and headstrong. I personally think if she meets the right man she would be an angel and a loving and caring wife."

"I doubt any man would want to try to tame her, she's not very polite."

His aunt flicked the dishcloth at him. "That's not very nice; every woman deserves a good man."

"But you just said she will never settle..."

"Oh bother, don't mind what I said, I'm telling you now, the man who marries her would be the luckiest man alive."

His aunt winked at him and John rolled his eyes. His aunt was up to something and he wasn't so sure if he would play along.

"So tell me, are you still enjoying working as a Policeman?"

John crossed his arms and leaned on the table, "I'm a detective, but yes, I enjoy it."

"It must be terrible to have to witness all the crimes in the city and having to face all those ruthless criminals every day."

John couldn't agree more. Sometimes his job took him from one extreme to the next, but he enjoyed his job, especially when he gets to put criminals behind bars, while contributing to making the world a better place.

"It's not all that bad Aunt Mae, some good things also come from the work I do; it's very rewarding when you get to save lives."

His aunt cupped his hand and smiled softly at him. "I'm just so worried about you John; I can't bear the thought of ever losing you. You're all I have left."

John held his aunt's hand and patted it gently. He wanted to promise her he would be safe but he couldn't. In his line of work, it was the one promise he could never make. But for the time being he was here, and once she is settled with Mable at the neighbouring farm, she wouldn't feel so lonely.

Chapter 3

The buggy bounced over the dirt road towards the market. While Faith steered, Becky clung to the tray of scones and cakes her grandmother had baked.

"Do you think we would sell anything today?" her sister asked curiously.

"Of course, why wouldn't we, I used *mamm's* recipe for the scones, and the people enjoyed her baking."

"Yes but we usually sell cream with the scones."

"So today we have cheese and strawberry jam, it's something different. And we also have the vegetables and the eggs."

Faith knew all too well that Becky was nervous about her wedding arrangements, and although the wedding was a simple affair and there were no real frills about it, it was catering for the community that may put them out of pocket. But either way, she would not allow a simple fox to ruin her sister's happiest day. She looked at Becky and smiled. "Trust me, we'll manage."

"I hope so."

"Anyway, once I've set up the table, and everyone else who comes to the market pays for their tables, you'll see we'll have plenty to be grateful for."

"But most of it will go to the church."

"And we'll still have plenty."

It had been Faith's idea to set up an Amish market not too far from town, where Amish farmers could sell their produce. It formed a great part of the rest of the tourist attractions Lancaster County had. From visiting the oldest Amish home to the blacksmith, the market was a place where tourists and locals could buy speciality Amish foods, handmade furniture and trinkets and even quilts. Each stall owner had to pay a levy to hire a spot. Since she owned the market, she got to take some of the proceeds home, whilst the stall owners gained from their own profits. When the idea first came to her, she was concerned that the council would turn her down. But to her surprise they didn't. Bishop Fischer, a good friend of her *grossmammi* had thought it to be a brilliant idea and if it wasn't for him who convinced the others, she would still fight to make ends meet.

Along the street where the market stalls lined the sidewalks, buggies stood one next to the other. Faith found a spot to stand her buggy and climbed out, taking the tray of scones from Becky.

"Why don't you go find Caleb and ask him to come and help us carry all the vegetables to the stall," she said.

Becky skipped off, and Faith smiled. Her little sister was like a fresh breeze, especially when she got to see Caleb. For a moment she wondered what it would be like to fall in love, but that thought was fleeting. After all she had to endure, watching her mother die; she couldn't even imagine falling in love.

In no time, they had everything set up. The rest of the stall owners had paid their dues and already tourists were flocking into the market.

"Faith!" she heard someone call her name.

She looked up to find Mae rolling up to her stall in her wheel chair, behind her, the young man she saw a few mornings ago. Her heart fluttered in her chest and she held her breath.

"Hello Mae, what a lovely surprise."

She avoided looking at the young man but only because she couldn't stand the way he made her feel.

"I believe you've met my nephew, John Collins the other morning."

Faith's breath left her in, and she looked up at him, "John?"

"In the flesh," he grinned. "Don't worry, I also didn't recognize you."

Embarrassed, Faith wiped her hands and offered a smile. "I'm sorry about the other morning; I didn't mean to be so..."

"No need to apologize," he interrupted. "You had your hands full with that fox."

His smile tugged at her and she felt a blush spread from her neck up to her cheeks.

"Yes, they seem to sneak in quite often, I honestly don't know what to do anymore."

He made her feel clumsy, especially now that she knew who he was. From as early as she could remember as a young girl, she always secretly fancied the young boy who occasionally visited Mae. She used to hide in the bushes and watch him play with his trucks, often hoping he would ask her to join him. But even if he did, her daed would never have allowed it. He was always just out of reach.

Mae wheeled her chair to the next stall leaving John alone with her and an awkward silence fell between them.

"I'm surprised to see you're still here," John said just as Faith spoke. "So where have you been all this time?"

They laughed and John rubbed the back of his neck, "I'm a detective now, I've just come to help my aunt to sell her farm."

Curiosity got the better of her and she asked, "What made you decide to become a detective?"

He shrugged, stepped out of the way of one of the tourists browsing the stall, and then continued, "My gut told me to, the world is in need of people who can try to make it a better place."

She laughed and rolled her eyes, "Only if God wills it."

"And why wouldn't He? Surely He would want the man who killed your father to be punished."

Faith's blood ran cold. Of course she wanted him punished, but it wasn't up to her to see to that, and for John to make such a statement was almost cruel. She turned away from him, took over the order Becky was handling and served the customer.

"Faith, I'm sorry, that was uncalled for."

She busied herself with rearranging some of the scones, avoiding his gaze. "It is not up to me to call any man to judgement, and it is not up to you either. Only God can Judge man's sins."

When John didn't respond she looked up at him, his expression saddened.

"Is it not God who judges?" she asked again.

John stepped closer to the table and reached as if he was about to take her hand then withdrew it and said, "Let every person be subject to the governing authorities. For there is no authority except from God, and those that exist have been instituted by God."

Faith half stumbled back. She recognized the scripture immediately and her heart ached. If God was the one who instituted governing authorities why could her father's killer not have been brought to justice?

"Let me take you home later, we have a lot to talk about," he said interrupting her thoughts when she didn't respond.

Half shocked she glanced up at him and blinked, "Take me home?"

Smiling he nodded, "Yes, I'll take you home."

She laughed and turned away, hiding her blush, "I have to get Becky home and I doubt you'll be able to steer the horses."

"You seem to forget," he chuckled, "I grew up on a farm. I can take you home in your own Buggy."

John didn't wait on her response, he smiled, placed some money on the table, took a scone and walked away to meet up with his aunt, leaving Faith gaping after him.

"I think the Englischer likes you," Becky nudged her side.

Faith shoved the money into the money pouch and clicked her tongue. "That's utter nonsense. He's an Englischer; they don't care for simple women."

"Ah, so you do fancy him!" her sister laughed.

"I most certainly... most definitely do not!" Faith protested, but even as she did, she knew she was lying.

Chapter 4

Curiosity and intrigue were the driving forces behind John's determination to get to know Faith better. Before now, he had been quite happy living the single life, especially considering his line of work. Too often in the past had he witnessed cops dying in the line of duty, leaving behind loved ones, and he never, for one moment thought he would consider the prospect of actually dating someone. But here he was, and to make matters worse, she was Amish. It was an unrealistic notion to say the least and of the little he knew about them, one thing was sure, they didn't like state law, they did not like weapons and they did not like Englischers, not much anyway.

It's been a week since he asked to offer her a ride home, and since then they had both fallen into this peculiar habit. Each day he got to learn more about her, yet there was so much that remained undiscovered and time was running out. In a week's time his business here would be concluded and he would have to head back home to the city.

He stood waiting beside her buggy late on the Friday afternoon, and when she spotted him an unspoken moment of truth passed between them. Her eyes met his, and he an ache formed deep in the pit of his stomach, because he knew goodbye wasn't far beyond the horizon.

"Hello John," she smiled as she walked up to him, a basket hanging in the crook of her arm.

"Hello," he smiled and stepped aside for her to get into the buggy.

Speculative and even judging glances didn't escape his attention, but if those stares did not seem to bother Faith, he would not let them trouble him either. He wasn't doing anything he shouldn't and her virtue was as intact as the gears of a working clock.

"I hope you don't mind, but I thought we could take a bit of a detour?" he suggested.

Faith gave him a shy smile and nodded, "I don't mind, but where would you be going?"

"I just thought it would be a nice change, I want to show you something, and it's on my aunt's farm."

When she looked his way from under her lashes, he saw something hidden behind the windows of his soul that both pleased and frightened him and all he could do was return her smile.

He pulled up to the farmhouse and helped Faith out of the buggy.

"This way," he said and led her around the back of the house to the big Cedar tree.

"Oh goodness, that's the treehouse you used to play in!" she exclaimed as they got closer.

He chuckled, "You remember the treehouse then?"

She skipped ahead and turned, walking backwards, "You used to sit up in the tree and spy on us."

That nugget of information surprised him, and he dragged a hand through his hair. He always thought he had gone unnoticed back when he was a kid.

"Wait here, I want to show you something."

The treehouse was much lower to the ground, now that he was all grown up. As a kid it always felt as if he was high up in the sky. In two quick lifts he was level with the structure, which over time had decayed and was definitely no longer suitable for anyone to try out. He over the edge of the floor and pulled a small box closer before leaping to the ground.

"What do you have there?" she asked curiously as she peeked over his hands into the box.

"My treasures I kept here for when I came to visit."

"You kept treasures?"

"Yep, I did." He opened the lid and in it were a few toy cars, marbles and baseball cards. "Ah here we go."

He pulled out a small pocket bible and handed it to her and smiled. "I actually got this from your dad. He caught me sneaking around your barn and I got such a fright, I thought he was going..."

"My father gave you this?" she interrupted. Her fingers trembling as she opened it up on the first page.

Even her voice seemed to tremble and John had to fight the urge to comfort her. "He did, he thought or rather hoped, the bible would give me some direction. I thought you would want to have it."

She was silent, and by the way her bottom lip wobbled and her chest rose and fell, he knew she was fighting against the flood gates that threatened to burst open.

"Thank you," she whispered.

"No need to thank me, your dad was a good man."

A sob escaped her and impulsively John reached for her, but instead she shoved the bible into his chest and stepped away, tears filling her eyes. "I should not be here, we cannot be friends."

"Faith, I..."

"No," she blurted. "I don't want to hear anything, I—I have to go."

She didn't give him any chance to respond, instead rushed across the field towards her buggy.

He knew the moment he reached for her, that he had overstepped his boundaries, but it was only his natural instinct to comfort her. But she was right. They couldn't be friends because what he felt for her moved far beyond friendship and the chasm between their lives and beliefs were far too wide to bridge. Disheartened, angry and frustrated he headed to the house instead. By Monday, he would finalize the sale of his aunt's farm and then hire a removal company to come and help her move her belongings into storage.

Chapter 5

Finally, he could avenge his brother's death and show the detective exactly how it feels to lose someone you love.

He'd been searching for Detective Collins for over four months, and after being on a wild goose chase he finally managed to track him down. When his brother was sentenced to thirty years in ADX Maximum Security Prison, he had been determined to appeal the sentence, but his brother never saw the light of another day. No thanks to Collins his younger brother never made it past the first week. His bloodied body was discovered by one of the guards in the showers. Stabbed multiple times with his hand and feet hogtied behind his back like an animal. He didn't care what anyone said, his brother was innocent. The death of the young student was an accident and his brother was a pawn, used to cover the truth of what really happened.

Brian Gregson waited patiently as the young woman walked towards the door. Through the living room window, he had a bird's-eye view of the front gate. Today, innocent blood will be spilled and there was nothing anyone would do about it. Collins will suffer just like he had suffered.

The old woman sat bound to the chair, her mouth gagged.

"It's not too long now," he whispered as he hooked the curtain with one finger and glanced outside. "It's a pity you came home when you did. This could all have been avoided."

The woman sobbed and tried to wriggle free and Brian simply ignored her. He refused to let his humanity overrule his decision this time, his humanity died with his brother.

"*Grossmammi*, have you seen B..."

Faith's words faded as fear gripped her heart and squeezed the air out of her lungs. Before she could utter a cry, the man with the leather gloves grabbed her violently, clasping his one hand over her mouth and the other around her arms pinning her to his body.

"Don't make a single sound," he warned her as he dragged her to where her *grossmammi* sat.

Terrified that he would harm them she did exactly what he said. He bound her hands with a piece of cloth and tugged them so tight it constricted the blood flow to her fingers. *God, why is this happening again,* she prayed silently, tears stinging her eyes. The intruder dumped her on to the sofa and pointed a gun at her and she flinched.

"Please, you don't have to do this," she pleaded with him.

"You don't get to tell me what I can and cannot do," he growled. "When are you expecting Collins?"

Confusion etched on her face she frowned, "Collins?"

Waving the gun in the air he muttered, "Don't play dumb with me woman, the detective, when are you expecting him?"

She shook her head furiously. "I don't know he never comes here..."

"Lies, I've seen him here." Sweat beaded on the intruder's brow and, and saliva gathered at the corners of his mouth. He went from raging to laughing menacingly at her. "I've been watching the two of you for days, and I can see the way he looks at you."

"No you're wrong," she protested, "He's an Englischer, it's not like that."

He huffed and spun around to walk to the window. "You tell yourself that."

From the corner of her eye, Faith spotted a movement in the kitchen. It was Becky and her heart stopped. No! She looked back at the intruder who was still standing with his back to her and then shook her head towards Becky. He may harm her or her *grossmammi* but she would fight tooth and nail to protect her sister.

The intruder spun around and Faith jumped, crawling back on to the sofa. "Please, I don't know what you want with the detective but if it's him you want, but please don't hurt my grandmother," she begged. "She's old."

"That's just too bad aint it? Unfortunately, she was in the wrong place at the wrong time."

"If you can just tell me what it is you..."

"Quiet!" He banged the heels of his palms against the sides of his head, "You're nagging is really starting to annoy me."

Faith sunk deeper into the couch, her mind racing. Becky was no longer in the kitchen, and she could only hope her sister went to get help. Images of that fateful night when her father was murdered, also by an intruder and it was as if history was repeating itself and all she could do was pray for God to intervene.

Chapter 6

"John! John Collins!"

The frantic banging on the door rang through the house like a reign of bullets and John rushed to open it before his aunt woke up. Both surprised and shocked to see Becky looking like she had seen a ghost he grabbed her by her shoulders.

"Becky calm down, what is it?"

Trying to catch her breath and waving her hand towards the house, he couldn't make out a think she was saying.

"Come inside and calm down, what's gotten you so upset?"

"No! Hurry – someone – house – Faith," she blurted incoherently.

"What about Faith, is she hurt?" Panic threatened his otherwise composed demeanour.

"Gun – there's a man with a gun!" Becky finally managed to say before she collapsed and he caught her just in time.

A man with a gun in Faith's house... the weight and the reality of the situation cut through him like a two edged sword and he went cold. The thought of Faith being hurt is bad enough, but the thought of her being shot and killed drove him to the brink of insanity.

"Keep it together Collins," he told himself as he helped Becky into the house.

"John?" his aunt called from her room, "What is that racket?"

"Nothing Nan, it's just Becky from next door." He didn't want to worry his aunt right this minute; she was fragile as it was.

He gently lay Becky on the couch and walked to the window. Through the lace curtains it was easy to see the farmhouse where the intruder held Faith, knowing he won't be visible from the outside. He had to figure out a way to get to the house without being detected. Night had already fallen and if he was careful enough, he could make it around the back and get to the house. A sob behind him drew his attention, and he knelt down before Becky.

"Where in the house is he holding Faith?" he asked.

She swallowed, "In the living room, he has my *grossmammi* too, they are tied up, you have to go help them."

"I will, I just need to be careful. What type of gun does he have?"

Her bottom lip trembled, and she wiped the tears from her cheeks, "I don't know, it's a gun, he's looking for the detective."

Shock ricocheted through him like an atomic blast, flattening everything in his wake.

"What does he look like?"

She shook her head, "I don't know, I couldn't see him, I could only hear him."

"Did he have an accent?"

"I don't know!" Faith cried.

John pinched the bridge of his nose and took a few controlling breaths. He had no real profile to go by, but if this man was looking for him, it must have been someone he crossed swords with on the streets before.

He took Becky's hands and squeezed them. "Is there anything at all you can remember, did he say why he wanted me?"

She looked at him and the fear was evident in her eyes. "All he wanted to know is when Faith is expecting you. Please you have to go help them."

John stood and walked back to the window, glanced towards the farmhouse. It was obvious, whoever it was, was expecting him to go there. Maybe he can talk the intruder down and make some sort of deal, his life for Faith's. He's had to deal with hostage situations before, successfully too, but this was different. This was aimed at him and Faith and her grandmother's life was in peril.

"OK, Becky, I need you to take my phone, it has no signal here, but if you go up the road to the railway crossing, you should be able to call 911 from there."

She nodded anxiously and clutched his phone in her hand.

"You need to move along the tree-line where he can't spot you."

"But what if he kills…"

"That will not happen, I will get your grandmother and Faith to safety, but I need you to do exactly as I said. As soon as you see me walk across the field, you go for help. Can you do that?"

She gulped and nodded, "Yes, yes I can."

"OK, now wait until you see me."

He squeezed her hands and stood up. He had never been one to pray, but tonight desperation drove him to just that. As he walked across the field towards the farmhouse, he kept praying that God would intervene. A few hours ago, he was ready to leave this place and Faith behind, but now, the thought of losing her was terrifying.

Chapter 7

A deathly silence hung in the atmosphere. The intruder guarding the window while tapping the gun against his leg. While he wasn't watching them, she used her teeth to untie her hands and praying for a miracle.

"Ah! I knew he would come sooner or later!"

Faith jumped and tucked her hands on her lap, pretending to be bound.

"What do you want with him?" she asked nervously.

The intruder smirked, his eyes cold and calculated. "I want him to feel my pain, to see what it is to lose someone he loves. I want him to watch you die and then I want to plant a bullet in his brain."

Faith froze, her heart felt as if it was about to jump out of her throat. He wanted to kill her? "God have mercy," she whispered.

"No mercy will be coming your way sweetheart, just like no mercy came my brother's way."

"Please I beg…"

"Shut up!" he roared, pressing the cold steel barrel of the gun against her head.

His breath reeked of garlic and alcohol and Faith held her breath, unable to move an inch.

The intruder swept towards the window and a cruel smile played on his lips. He took his position behind the door, gut in one hand and his other hand on the door handle. The moment John knocked on the door; he flung it open and wielded his gun in Johns face. Faith couldn't help the shriek that escaped her and she moved closer to her *grossmammi*.

"John Collins, it's about time," he spat, "Do come in, and I suggest you try nothing.

Faith met John's serious gaze and him not showing any surprise only meant one thing. Becky.

"John!" Faith cried out.

"Shut up woman! You will speak when you're spoken to don't you have any respect for the superiority of man?"

"Brian, whatever it is you're here for, I'm sure we can settle this as two grown men."

He knew the man, Faith realized.

The intruder chuckled, and pointed the gun at John, "We have a debt to settle, your girlfriend's life for my brother's."

"How will taking her life bring your brother back?"

"He should never have been sent to prison, he was innocent!"

John's hands were in the air, but he stood with the composure of a bishop and looked past the intruder at her.

"You know that isn't true, Rob was responsible for the girl's death, his DNA was all over the crime scene."

"He loved her! He would never have killed her!"

Faith's head was spinning, all of this was over a crime committed by another man and now that man's brother has come to avenge him. For a moment her better nature almost felt sorry for Brian. She too wanted to avenge her father's death once, but she realized soon enough that vengeance was never the answer.

"It was a crime of passion."

"You liar!" Brian shouted.

John was trying to rile him up, it was obvious, and Faith wasn't so sure if John's plan would even work. If he kept up with this, she would be dead in no time.

"Brian, listen to me, she cheated on your brother and your brother couldn't stand it. It may not have been intentional, but he was found guilty of premeditated murder, he confessed."

"They could have pleaded temporary insanity, reduced his sentence to manslaughter, but they gave him thirty years, and he survived one week! Do you know what they did to him when they killed him?"

"That was unfortunate..." John started.

He had hardly spoken when Brian exploded and launched himself towards John. Everything happened so fast, John tackled him and they both crashed on to the floor. During the scuffle the gun slid across the floor and it was then when Faith knew it was now or never.

She leaped across the floor and dove for the gun, snatching it up off the floor. The cold steel felt like death in her trembling hands and she pointed it haphazardly at the two men rolling around and punching each other.

"Stop or I'll shoot!"

They didn't pay her any notice, and she raised the gun in the air and pulled the trigger. A shot rang out and shards of ceiling board splintered and fell to the floor.

"I said stop it!"

Both men stopped and in a blink of an eye John had Brian pinned face down on the floor with the man's arms wedged behind his back and his knee pressing against him. In the distance the sound of sirens were drawing closer, but Faith couldn't let the gun go. Filled with such uncontainable anger, with her finger on the trigger she kept it pointed at Brian.

"Faith," John said calmly. "Give me the gun."

She couldn't move, she wouldn't, all she could think of was how ruthless the man was and how he had threatened to kill both her and her *grossmammi*.

"Faith, give me the gun."

John's voice filtered into her mind and then the sound of the sirens became clearer. As if everything had slowed down, she dropped the gun in John's hand. Becky barged in from the kitchen and flung herself at her *grossmammi*. Suddenly the police were everywhere. John had apprehended the intruder and handed him over. A medical person came and wrapped a blanket around her shoulders and led her outside to the ambulance. Everywhere around them onlookers from the community had gathered. The realisation of what had happened and of what could have happened had finally surface and everything faded in and out of vision until everything around her grew as black as night.

Chapter 8

The early morning air was crisp and soft breeze rustled the leaves as Faith made her way to the barn to milk the cow. Her life had been irrevocably changed, and after the whole ordeal with the intruder she wasn't so sure if she would ever be the same. But life had to go on. John ended up having to return to the city, and she was left to pick up the pieces. Becky finally married Caleb and her little sister was happier than ever. As for her *grossmammi*, her health had taken a knock, and she knew it wouldn't be long before she would have to say farewell.

As she pulled the stool closer and placed the bucket under the cow she wiped away a tear. Life wasn't fair, but she knew with God's grace and guidance she would find the strength to get through anything.

"Well Molly, soon enough it would just be you and me," she said to the cow and stroked its side. "But we'll make it, you'll see."

"Do all Amish woman talk to cows when they milk them?"

The sound of John's voice jolted Faith, and she leapt to her feet, sending the bucket flying.

"John! You scared me!" she scolded.

At the same time she stood like a statue, not sure what to do. He was dressed like one of them, in Amish clothes. From the plain brown pants to the brim hat and suspenders and she wasn't quite sure what to make of it.

He chuckled and spread his arms. "So what do you think does it suit me?"

Frowning she studied him and said, "What are you wearing?"

His smile softened, and he closed the distance between them, stopping barely a foot away from her.

"I'm hoping to redeem myself and trusting that you can find it in your hear to forgive me for being such a fool."

"I don't understand," she whispered, her breath catching in her throat. "There is nothing to forgive."

He reached as if wanting to touch her, but stopped and took his hat off instead.

"I caused you much pain, but after almost losing you and realizing that I want peace and serenity in my life, I knew I could only find it with you. Now I know," he said and then took her hand in his, "I know I'm not as Amish as everyone else, but I want to try, because if I have to live one more day wondering about the what-ifs and what-nots, I will go insane."

She tilted her head, a familiar flutter starting at the bottom of her stomach and working its way up to her heart. "What are you trying to day John?"

He took a breath, exhaled slowly and then bent down on one knee.

"I know it's not an Amish custom, but while I'm still learning, I want to do this right. Faith Bontrager, would you marry me?"

If she was any weaker a woman, her legs would have given out from under her. Just yesterday she was trying to forget John and move on with her life. And now here he was in front of her, asking for her hand in marriage.

"Are you certain you want to do this?" she asked hesitantly, "Being Amish isn't an easy feat."

He remained on his knee and nodded, "The dress code is something getting used to, but I'm in love with you Faith, and where you go, I go."

Faith's eyes shot full of tears and she fell to her knees in front of him. Just then Becky, Caleb and her *grossmammi* jumped out from behind the wall and clapped and cheered.

"I had to ask them first," he admitted and rested his forehead against hers. "I could kiss you now, but I think that's against the rules."

She laughed and cupped his face, "I'll pray for forgiveness after," and pressed her lips against his.

Her heart soared to new heights, and for the first time since she can remember, she felt the presence of God, really felt it. Love and joy flooded her soul. He had intervened through faith and trust, and He had brought her a man who would cherish and protect her against the wickedness of the world.

Romans 8:28
And we know that God causes all things to work together for good to those who love God, to those who are called according to His purpose.

amish sunday

It was a beautiful Sunday, and Bridget woke at the sound of the crowing rooster. The sun filtered through the curtains like warm liquid, and splashed Bridget's face with a welcome warmth. There were still hours left until church, and Bridget stretched luxuriously in bed, smiling. Then suddenly - a loud crash. Bridget's smile fell. The children were awake.

Bridget lived in a sturdy Amish house that her great-grandfather had built in the 70's, with her father and six siblings. Her mother had died in childbirth leaving Bridget, the oldest, to take care of the domestic affairs while the younger boys helped their father in the fields. She sighed. She hated when the children woke before her.

"Good morning, Papa," she said cheerfully as she entered the living room fully dressed, her plain clothes firmly secured with hooks and pins, hair pulled back in a modest bun. Her father grunted in reply, staring down at a handwritten letter.

Bridget worriedly noted the gray tinge to his face - he'd been getting sicker and sicker. Last month he nearly collapsed, clutching his heart. But the village doctor passed away almost four months ago, and his apprentice, a fourteen year old boy, had almost killed the little Bram baby by forgetting to wash his cut before dressing it.

Bridget stoked the fire while her sisters played with straw dolls on the floor. She scolded one of them, "Lydia, stop that foolishness and get me a bucket of water."

Bridget's father looked up from the letter and chuckled. "You sound like your mother when you talk to that girl."

"Maybe it's because she reminds me of myself," replied Bridget wistfully, watching the her little girl with long briads scamper to the well.

A sudden rumble sounded from above the road, Bridget cursed under her breath and then winced, hoping her father hadn't heard. He looked at her sharply, but said nothing - just a warning this time, then.

"It's those Robinsons," he explained, "those traitors and their tourists."

The Robinsons were a young family of terrible farmers; their crops died on the vine, every year. To supplement their income, they had begun riding their buggy to the nearby city (more a town, really), picking up elementary schoolers and their teachers for educational field trips. This was widely seen as the most disastrous sort of betrayal. No one could bear the thought of those godless children, with their grimy bare hands, touching the Robinsons' prized cows, churning their butter, picking their corn.

Bridget clucked her tongue, "I swear their milk will go sour while it's still in the cow if they go on like this."

"Some people are shameless," agreed her father.

"Sister Bridget?" a voice piped in. It was Lydia, precariously shouldering the cauldron full of water. "I think there's something wrong with Bessie, she keeps licking her shoulder."

"I'll look at it after breakfast," Bridget said.

The oatmeal bubbled over the fire and the children lined up with their wooden bowls.

"We're getting a new doctor," Paul said, looking almost nervous.

Bridget frowned. Something was up - her father was a strong man, a farmer and a good man. He had saved the farm from the brink of destruction by financial ruin and poor weather many a time. She had rarely seen him look as unsure as he did at that moment. She raised one eyebrow.

"And? Anyone we know?"

"It's Amos," answered Paul grimly, and Bridget felt the ground under her rumble. Her vision flattened into a thin circle, and she swallowed nervously.

"I thought he was done with us. He thought we were *backwards*. That he needed to get out. That he..." she trailed off.

"That he would rather die than marry an Amish girl," finished Paul. The details of that infamous last line had resounded through the town, and even now, five years later, remained fresh in everyone's mind.

"So he's really coming back?"

"Yes," confirmed Paul. "Listen, Bridget-"

"I know what you're going to say."

"There are a lot of eligible young men in the town. Adam, Gabriel, all fine, strong men who would love and provide for you. Amos may be settling back here now, but don't forget that he left the church, he left the people who needed him. He left you."

"I know, Papa," Bridget frowned for a second. "But I think you should go to him, when he comes."

Paul opened his mouth as if to argue, when a deep hacking cough emerged from the back of his throat.

"I'll go to him, Bridget, I'll let him fix me up. But that doesn't mean I trust him."

After that, there was no more talk of Amos. Together, the children, Bridget, and Paul ate their oatmeal which was mixed with brown sugar and huckleberries. The little wood chime that Lydia had made tinkled enchantingly in the spring breeze. The corn was rising from the ground in tender shoots, the cows were healthy and full of milk to be pumped from ripe udders. Down the road, Bridget knew, were many handsome, well-mannered men who were clamoring to talk to her, dance with her, maybe even give her a chaste kiss on the hand or lips.

It was a beautiful, perfect morning in a beautiful, perfect life.

Bridget wasn't about to let Amos ruin it for her.

By the time Bridget got her sisters and brothers ready for church, wrangling the boys into starch collared shirts, the girls into long cotton dresses, they were almost late.

"Hurry *up*, Bridget," Paul tapped his foot impatiently. Even with his straw hat drawn low and his collar pulled up severely around his chin, he looked weak, sickly. Bridget had a brief moment of intense fear as she looked at him. "*Bridget*," he scolded, and she snapped out of it.

She ferried the children out the door, and they piled into the carriage while Bridget and her father sat up front. Bridget drove, holding the whip - unconventional, yes, but with her father's weakening muscles, the family had no choice.

The church was tall and white, built and rebuilt by the hands of many generations working together. Today, it was strung with flowers - it is the first day of fall, and the town was celebrating.

"So good to see you," said Paul to the passing Maribel family, who were huffing on foot because their horse had thrown a hoof. A young man, sweetly handsome, caught Bridget's eyes and smiled warmly but demurely. Bridget looked away, flattered; Eliot was the most eligible bachelor in town.

After tying their horses to the picket fence, Bridget and her family lined into the pew, and settled in to listen to the sermon. Father Mathews was a gentle speaker, far more sweet-spoken than most speakers. Bridget was somewhat sinfully in the habit of letting his voice carry her into the fields, away from the substance of the sermon and into a welcoming half-sleep.

"We must be conscious of the beauty around us, for beauty is not something to be squandered. Beauty is God's gift, and we must never let it go without seeking to return."

Bridget became aware of a rustling on the other side of the pew. A man was turning and looking at her. This was met with a ripple of frowns throughout the congregation - these were people who had mastered stillness. Bridget looked out of the corner of her eye at the sudden movement.

Amos; thick brown hair that swept in curls over his forehead, high cheekbones, a chin with the strength of earth. He had become handsomer, more of a man, with thick dark stubble around his lip and beard, and what seemed like an additional layer of strength and muscle over his already tall and strong body.

Amos. Bridget saw herself as he might see her; red-haired as always, with wide hips and a healthy bust, a face peppered with child-like freckles. The same as always, if a bit more exhausted. She squirmed in her seat.

"...And we welcome back into our midst the young Amos, who has seen the error of his ways and has returned once more to his community, his family. Have you anything to say, Amos?"

And Bridget watched as he turned his gaze away from her and spoke loud and clear to the congregation: "I left thinking that I had no need of the things that made me who I am; the friends, hard work, and devotion to God that I was raised with, that raised me. I return now, to offer my services as a man of medicine. I may not have acquired my skills through honest, Amish ways, but I hope that I can save at least one life, and through that life become closer to the God I abandoned."

There was some impressed raising of eyebrows at this. The boy spoke well. Lydia, sitting besides Bridget, hissed, "he speaks like a city boy," but she was the only one who was unimpressed. Bridget felt her past and her grievances fall into the well of Amos' words. Amos, who she once knew so well.

After the church, the entire congregation headed to the yard for butter, bread and cheese, spread out on long linen tables. Because it was first fall, the church had also slaughtered a cow, and the smell of fat hitting the fire began to waft into the air.

Bridget rushed through the busy, happy, bodies, trying to find her father.

"Aren't you staying?" asked a voice, concerned.

"Oh, I..." answered Bridget, before rushing away. When she found her father, she half collided with him.

"Can we *go*?" she asked, seething.

Paul looked at his daughter one moment, the anxiety that peppered her unknowingly beautiful face. "In a moment, baby."

Bridget winced. Paul only called her baby when he was particularly worried about her, or when he thought she had been overworked. He sidestepped her gently and walked towards Farmer Gibbons, with whom he was negotiating a deal for a new horse.

She stood there for a long minute, staring at the spring time joy on people's faces, and feeling utterly and completely alone.

Then, suddenly, a hand on her shoulder. Bridget spun around and looked up into the face of - she wasn't even surprised - Amos.

"Listen, Bridget," he paused. Against her better judgement, she looked up at the full force of his face. His face looked so masculine and beautiful in that moment, his strong cheekbones glowing in the sun. His eyes were the deepest black, eyes she could find herself or lose herself in, and in those eyes she saw the past three years as if through a backwards facing mirror. She saw his pain, his agony, and her own.

But that first eye contact, after so many years, was too much. She ran away before he could say another word, busying herself among the children. For the rest of the feast Amos watched her work, kneeling down to take part in the children's imaginary games. She had suffered so much in his absence. The death of her mother, her father's illness.

But she hadn't married. Amos held onto that. She hadn't married.

Weeks passed. Paul went to see Amos, who gave him a medicine made from ground roots and herbs. Bridget sat firmly in the waiting room, lowering her eyes when Amos exited the small office to tell her his diagnosis.

"I'm sure my father will be able to fill me in just fine," she said, and that was all. This time, she did not make the mistake of eye contact.

Later, in the buggy, she asked her father how he had seemed.

Paul grunted. "Like a perfectly fine doctor. But don't be fooled, Bridget. He will always be a traitor."

They passed weeks like this, Bridget refusing to make eye contact every time she passed Amos in community gatherings or church events. Until, on the day of the first frost, their only cauldron cracked a leak an hour before dinner time.

"I know we should have replaced it earlier," said Bridget, mentally cursing her father for his stinginess.

"Don't worry, dear," said Paul, "I'll go."

But Bridget's father had recently taken turn for the worse, and he looked grey and pinned down in the bed. She gently but firmly pushed him back into the bed, then vanished into her room to pull on her best woolen dress.

"I'll go," she said. Her father began to protest - it wasn't proper for a young lady to travel by herself in growing snowfall. Some would argue, not allowed.

But Bridget gave her father a stern and determined look. Paul said nothing, taken aback. She was growing far too headstrong to make a good Amish wife. This must, he thought, be the result of Amos's brief reappearance. He made a mental note to begin looking for husbands as soon as he possibly could.

"At least take Lydia with you," he shouted after her retreating back, but she was already gone.

By herself, Bridget attached the horse to the buggy and pulled herself up. She tapped the horse lightly on the shoulder with a whip, and it responded immediately, treading gently on the half-frozen ground. As they turned out of the small country road to the larger one, Bridget saw that it was snowing harder than she thought, and the snow collected on the path in clumps that hardened immediately to ice. She kept one hand tight to the reigns, and the other on her whip, which she flicked gently and periodically. As she cantered along, Bridget thought, almost unwillingly, about Amos. How long could she keep avoiding him? Why wouldn't he just leave - he had before, hadn't he?

She closed her eyes, and saw the entire length of his body, modestly clad, the strong shoulders and chin. She unwillingly entered into a memory of her late childhood, when she was just becoming a woman, when they had spoken for hours on the front porch, both neglecting farmwork, both of them smiling foolishly at each other. He had such a beautiful, broken, smile. She had been sure in that moment that she would grow up and marry that man.

She shook her head, eyes still closed. Tried to change his face in her mind to that of any of the other eligible bachelor's in town, even to the face of a model in a glossy magazine she had seen left by the road, where the Robinsons did their tours, but nothing worked.

She was trapped, she was...

CRASH. She was tilting, swaying, falling, crashing. Bridget realized that the horse had wandered off the street in her moment of contemplation. *How could you be so stupid*, she screamed at herself. In slow motion, she tumbled out of the buggy. The horse screamed and bucked at the wheel, which broke in two. Bridget felt a warm gash on her arm before the earth slid slowly away.

She awoke to the sensation of floating, almost dreamily. She was in someone's arms, her legs curled up near her chest, swaying weakly in the cold air. For a moment she felt fear - then a deep, blissful calm overtook her. The arms were strong and gentle. They did not mean her harm.

Dreamily, only slightly aware of a pain on her arm, she looked up at the face of her savior - to find herself caught in the bottomless black stare of the village doctor, the best memory of her childhood, the man who stole her heart. Amos. "Are you ok?" he asked, peering down into her face like he could fall into her.

His face suddenly threw Bridget into hysterics. She had tried so hard to avoid this man and now - to be swaddled in his arms like a *child*. "Let go of me!" she cried out, struggling swiftly and with uncharacteristic anger. "I'm *fine*. I can handle this, I can get Papa or Lydia or-"

As she struggled, her shift rose up her legs. Amos deftly pulled it back down with one hand, preserving her modesty. "Bridget. Bridget listen to me." His voice was warm and assertive.

She quieted. "Can you walk?" he asked her. She nodded, anger still rising red behind her eyes. Amos put her gently down.

"Thank you for your concern," she said coldly. "I should be going now." She looked around. The horse had run off, and the buggy knelt brokenly on the frozen ground, spokes snapped in half.

"Don't be ridiculous," said Amos, "My home isn't far from here. Let me patch you up - I have the materials."

Bridget looked at him, shocked. "You want me to go alone to your home? I don't know what you learned in the outside world but-" Amos looked like he was going to laugh, "-and *what* could possibly be so funny about this?" From her peripheral vision, she saw blood drop to the ground. She wasn't hurt badly, but there was a disproportionate amount of blood.

"I'm sorry," said Amos, "I didn't mean to laugh. But my mother is home, Bridget. I know you're not that kind of girl." A brief pause. "I wouldn't care so much about you if you were."

"That's *rich*, Amos," said Bridget. His name sounded disconcertingly familiar in her mouth, "You care about *me*? You care about your doctor's salaries and your outside girls and your-"

Amos cut her off again. "You have a right to be angry, I don't contest that. You have a right to never speak to me again. But if you'll never talk to me again - at least let me take care of your arm."

Bridget looked down at the dripping wound. It was two miles to her father's farm, which was a long way to travel in the snow with an open wound. And even once she arrived, they lacked the proper materials, the boiled gauze and sharp antiseptic. "Fine," she snapped, "lead the way."

As they walked through the snow, they looked almost comical. He walked so easily through the drifts, his hard boots pounding assuredly on the banks of snowfall. She, on the other hand was stumbling and disoriented, not from the pain on her arm, which was diminishing, but from pure anger. How dare he come back into her life like this? How dare he thwart all her attempts to be rid of him?

They approached Amos's house, which she had only visited once or twice in her childhood. It was rather small - their plot was tiny compared to Bridget and her father's. Amos's mother looked out from the front window, smiling toothlessly (she had lost all her teeth in a battle with jaundice as a teenager), and waving. Bridget waved back, smiling a little herself at the enthusiasm of the greeting.

"Oh, Bridget, it is so lovely to see you," said Amos's mother as soon as she crossed the threshold, "but oh! you've hurt yourself."

"It's nothing," assured Bridget, a little stiffly.

"My Amos will fix you up right away. Oh, it is lovely to see you two friends again."

"I don't know if you would call us friends," replied Bridget, embarrassed.

"Mother, don't smother the girl," called Amos from the other room, "Bridget, if you could come in here, please?"

Bridget nodded politely to Amos's mother and tentatively walked through the threshold. The next room was clearly Amos's office, where her father had been treated weeks before. Amos was holding a thin needle over the candle's flame. Bridget gulped, "what's *that* for?" she asked.

"That's a pretty nasty cut, Bridget," answered Amos, still concentrating, "it'll need stitches." He gestured absent-mindedly to the empty share besides him. "Sit down."

She did as he asked. When he was done sterilizing the needle, he sat down opposite her and held her forearm in one of his. He sewed her up methodically and carefully, not speaking. It hurt less than she thought, but it still hurt. It wasn't until he had begun dressing the wound that Bridget allowed herself to look around. The room was full of shelves and cabinets, full of gauze and water, antiseptic and some pills and bottles she had never seen before.

"Are those from out of town?" she asked, looking at some of those colorful pills, a mix of admiration and accusation in her voice.

Amos looked where she was pointing. "Some of them, yes."

"You know," Bridget said, "Old Doctor Gary didn't use anything from the outside world."

Amos shook his head. "I don't belong to the outside world, but it isn't as bad as people say. There's a lot of sin, yes, but they have the most incredible medicines. Things that can disappear a lifetime of pain in a single moment. The sin and solitude of that world disgusts me. But if their medicine can save even one of the people I love," his eyes flicked up to meet Bridget's, "then they're worth breaking a couple rules for."

"There are people who would expel you for that thought."

"There are more people who like having a doctor who knows what he's doing."

Bridge quieted. She could hear the sounds of Amos's mother rummaging in the kitchen, the sounds of slicing and boiling. It was near dinner time, and the cloudy sky had dimmed in its furious gray hue.

"If the outside world is so great," Bridget's voice broke, cracked in half, almost died. She continued in a whisper. "If the outside world is so great, why didn't you stay away?"

Amos was quiet for a long time. He had finished wrapping up Bridget's arm and ran his arms gently up and down the bandaged area. "Do you remember that summer when we were kids and we found the wild dog who had given birth in the woods?"

"I remember."

"Remember how I wanted to steal the puppies for ourselves. How great would it be to have our own puppies, I told you. And it really was a perfectly ordinary piece of cruelty for a child to partake in. I'm certain I wasn't alone in this."

"But I convinced you to leave them alone."

"You said that it wasn't our place to take these children from their mothers. You said they needed her."

"They did."

"You went home, then. And - you don't know this - I took one anyway. I kept it in my room so you wouldn't know. For three days. Until one day it looked at me, making sad little yelping sounds. I went down to the wood where I knew the dog lived, in that little hollow under the tree, and I put it down there. I waited for hours to make sure nothing attacked it. And, as the sun went under the horizon, the mother dog came back. It took the little one inside the hollow, and that was that."

"What's your point?" Asked Bridget, trying to be combative but failing at the soft sound of his voice.

"You have always been the better person," He clasped her hand in his and looked straight into her eyes," I left because I was selfish and stupid, and for the years I was out there I couldn't look at anything without seeing your face - the sun, dogs, I couldn't even smell grass."

"Then why didn't you come back *sooner*?" she asked, her voice in a hush. She had tightened her grip on his hand.

"I thought you would hate me for it. I thought I had lost you forever. But I know now that love never expires. You might never forgive me but I will never stop loving you. I - oh, lord forgive me - I want to marry you."

"You left me."

"I will never leave again."

"When my mother died I was alone."

"I want to spend the rest of my life making that up to you. Taking care of you. Providing you with comforts and children."

"Amos - how can I? After everything? How can I?" She was crying, hot tears tracking down her cheekbones.

"I know you love me too, undeserving as I am. I can't imagine a life without this love. Can you?"

Bridget was quiet. "I think I need to leave now. The snow's died down and It's only a couple miles to the farm. Papa will be getting worried."

"Ok," said Amos, helping her onto her feet. He gave her a cauldron to borrow (the purpose of her trip anyway) and a bottle of something to dab on the wound. At the door, Bridget suddenly spun around and drew herself close to his face. She could feel the heat of his chest and arms, tense as though poise for embrace.

"Amos," she said, her lips chapped from cold but still pink and shapely, "My father tells me that Eliot will propose marriage soon. What would you do if I said yes? Would you leave again?"

Amos let out a shaky breath. "No, Bridget. I would let you have your love and your family. But as long as you are in this town I will be here also. And if I cannot marry you, I will not marry." Amos shut the door gently, looking almost as surprised as Bridget at the truth of this sudden statement.

Bridget stood in the cold for a second longer, then began the long walk home.

"I'm not comfortable with you going to town by yourself any longer," Paul told Bridget from the sunken spot on the bed where he had been resting all weekend, "it's time you chose a husband."

He had been suspicious around her ever since she came home with no horse, no buggy, and a carefully bandaged arm. His suspicion grew, even though she retrieved and repaired the buggy by asking for help in town, even as she found the runaway horse grazing in a nearby pasture. It reached a boiling point two weeks after her injury, when she returned to Amos to have her stitches removed. "You're so good with fixing the animals' wounds," he said, "can't you take the stitches out yourself?"

She said nothing. And when she came back, Paul was waiting for her with a list of the most eligible bachelors'.

"The Sing is next week," Paul reminded her, "I told Eliot he could look forward to being there."

"Eliot?" asked Bridget, her voice fading slightly. Amos had removed her stitches in silence, and there in the candlelit darkness, each of his subtle touches felt like an eternal promise. Paul didn't know, but where she had previously taken such pains to avoid Amos, she now took pains to encounter him wherever she could. A dialogue of love had sprung up patchwork between them, made entirely of niceties exchanged in the marketplace, a door held open on the way to church, fierce eye contact made as their buggies passed on a busy road. Only once had they truly spoken; walking off together after church, not so far as to be scandalous.

"I don't know how you may still feel about me, but I can sense a softening in your eyes," Amos had whispered.

"I...I feel my anger giving. Leaving, slowly. I feel myself...believing you? Am I crazy?"

Amos smiled. "If you're this crazy already, I want to tell you something."

"What?"

"Next week at the Sing, I'm going to ask you to marry me."

"What? So soon?"

"It's still far too late," he leaned down, his mouth pink and parted slightly, and for a moment Bridget was happy to kiss, to be like the outside women who succumb so easily to love.

"Amos," she said, pushing away, "people will talk." She gathered her skirts up and picked her way towards the church.

"Bridget!" called Amos, "is that a no?" He could see in her eyes that it was not.

As Bridget stared down Paul, who had just suggested - no, commanded - her to dance with Eliot at the Sing, and by extension, to allow him to court her, marry her, fill her with children and take her into the house. She wasn't sure if she was ready to marry Amos. But she didn't know if she could marry at all.

"Papa," she said, "I don't know if I can-"

Paul interrupted her, "That you're what? Ready? You were ready enough to walk off with Amos into the woods last Sunday. You were ready enough to visit him *by yourself* to get your stitches out!"

"Would you have me untreated by the village doctor?" cried out Bridget, her voice almost cracking, "would you rather have me sick, dying, than see this man, who is not as bad as you might think?"

Paul waited until her crying subsided - she did not realize that she was crying, the tears had slipped out in a moment of panic. "Bridget," he said calmly, "Amos is not a good match for you. He is tainted by the outside world. Eliot is a good man, strong, he will provide for you."

"Why do I have to get married at all?" cried out Bridget.

"I have already done you a great injustice by keeping you at home. But Lydia is a capable child, on the cusp of womanhood. When you marry, she will be able to take over the farm, and her brothers can take over once she marries."

Bridget was silent.

"Bridget," repeated Paul, "do not lose faith. This boy has been sent down to tempt you. Eliot will give you peace."

The next few weeks passed quickly, with Bridget once again avoid Amos. He seemed distraught at the change, several times reaching towards her in an unseemly way that made people shake their heads as they past. She would dodge his outstretched hand. She hoped that by avoiding him so strenuously, he would get the message; he could no longer propose at the Sing.

The morning of the sing, she dressed in her best, most modest clothes. She braided her hair carefully, and even let Lydia string those braids with beads. It was a clear, cool morning. She went downstairs to see her father dressed as handsomely as ever, a little unsteady on his feet but proud and tall.

"This is an important day, Bridget," Paul said to her as they (they whole family) piled into the buggy and their long-suffering horse, unused to carrying so many at once, pulled out of the little road. Bridget said nothing, and watched the countryside sway past.

At the swing, the table was laden with the fruits of the harvest and fiddlers were tuning their instruments. Bridget sat gently on a seat while everyone else bustled about, chattering with their friends they hadn't seen in church. "Bridget!" shouted Lydia, "come make a daisy chain with me!"

Bridget smiled weakly. "Maybe later, dear."

Paul stood firmly by Bridget, looking stern. When Amos came to say hello, Pau shot him a look of such venom that he quickly backed off. But Bridget could see a steely will in his eyes. Then Eliot came to pay his respects. He was a nice boy, with a broad, almost goofy face.

"Good morrow, Bridget," he said, speaking in the old-fashioned tongue of their ancestors, "how are you on this beautiful day?"

"Well," answered Bridget, curtly. Eliot looked up nervously at Paul, and chuckled a bit. Paul gave him a reassuring pat on the shoulder.

"We'll talk later," he said, "there'll be plenty of time for you to get to know each other in the coming months." When Paul had left, he leaned down to catch Bridget's ear. "What's wrong with you, daugther?" he hissed, "this is a good man. Why do you scorn him?"

"Papa," started Bridget, her eyes brimming with tears, "I've realized something about who I want to marry. I've realized..."

"Time for the dance!" someone yelled from the other side of the field, and immediately there was a ruckus drowning out Bridget's small voice. The chair was practically yanked out from underneath her, and immediately there was a great rush of limbs and smiles. She numbly remembered her dancing steps, and was quickly swung from partner to partner; her father, the old horse doctor, then Eliot's dumbly smiling face.

"Isn't this lovely?" he yelled at her, "the two of us dancing together?"

But before she had a chance to reply, partners changed again, and she found herself spinning gently in a circle with Amos. He didn't say anything, but he gave her a long, low, look, a look of absolute love and pain, and in turn Bridget found her own pain surfacing beyond the music and the dance, and she wanted nothing more than to be alone with him for a while, to just sit with him and love him.

Suddenly, a voice rose above the crowd. "Excuse me!" shouted the lead fiddler, "I believe we have a special announcement to be made!"

Bridget looked at Amos, horrorstruck (and perhaps a little hopeful). "What did you-"

"It wasn't me," whispered Amos urgently, "Bridget, whatever happens-"

Bridget was suddenly yanked away by the strong arm of her father. As he pulled her through the crowds of people, she noticed his breath sounded ragged, tired, his lungs rising and falling with something close to a rattle. "Papa are you ok?" Paul did not answer, and instead thrust her into the middle of a small clearing the people had formed. Also at the middle, Eliot, who was on one knee.

"Bridget," he said (had his voice always been so nasal, so whiny?), "you may not know me well, but I have watched you from afar. I have seen your strength as you cared for your mother and your sisters, I have seen your gentle grace through suffering."

As he continued his monologue, Bridget looked around her. The men and women were smiling, nodding, so full of charity. "And I knew from that moment you would make a wonderful mother for my children," Bridget looked down at Eliot's upturned face. "No," she whispered, "no." Eliot didn't hear here, both those closest to her began muttering. She tried to catch Amos's eyes in the crowd, but she couldn't find him. "No!" she was screaming now, "I can't! I can't!"

There was a collected gasp. Eliot reeled back as though slapped. Bridget's father appeared suddenly near her, and held her face in his hands. "Bridget!" he shouted, "why do you shame me this way? Why do you-" he inhaled gaspingly, with terror. His knees buckled, his face turned blue.

"Papa, are you ok?" cried Bridget, as the knot of people grew ever tighter. Paul collapsed to the floor in a quivering heap. "Papa! Papa!" And then everything for her, too, went black.

Bridget woke up in her own home, awkwardly crunched into an armchair. Her father was asleep in the bed, strange machines hooked up to him. She jolted, then ran up to his body to make sure he was breathing. And he was; slowly, laboriously but breathing. She immediately tried to pull the tubes out of his arm.

"Bridget, no," said a voice. Amos walked through the open door, "leave him be."

"What are these things?" cried out Bridget, "what have you done to him?"

"These are modern appliances," said Amos. "I didn't want to use them, but today they saved your fathers life."

"What happened to him?" asked Bridget, less panicked now that she knew her father was safe.

"He had a heart attack, a minor one. Nothing that rest shouldn't fix. He'll have to eat healthier from now on, and exercise. But I think he has a good many years left in him."

Bridget looked down at her hands. "This is my fault," she said, "I love you, I know I do. It's the simplest thing in the world to me, but look what it's done to my father."

Amos looked away. "Bridget, I never meant to come between you and your duty. If I could take all of this back I would."

"You'd do no such thing," croaked a voice from the bed. Amos and Bridget both gasped in delight. Paul had opened his eyes. "If I could have a moment with my daughter, please."

"Of course," stuttered Amos, "anything you want."

When they were alone, Bridget knelt deeply by her fathers bed and took his hands in hers. "Papa, I am so sorry."

He reached across the bed and put his hand, tough from years of farm labor, on her head. "Child, it was wrong of me to put so much pressure on you. I see now that this Amos cares for you more than Eliot ever will."

"Why do you think that?" asked Bridget, frowning.

"Where is Eliot now? Amos is here, he made the decisions that had to be made, controversial as they are."

Bridget looked down, but Paul cupped her chin in his hand. "I'm tired, Bridget," he said, "I'm tired of keeping my daughter from having what she wants." Bridget stood up shakily, and her father smiled at her. Slowly, she kissed him on the forehead, and turned to where Amos was waiting for her.

"What did he say?" Amos asked anxiously.

"He said we could be together," Bridget's voice sounded far away to her. "He said he wants us to be happy."

"Bridget!" cried Amos, "That's great news!"

"But Amos!" she looked up at him, tears falling from her eyes, "I don't know if I'm ready yet."

Amos held her hands in his, and looked deep into her beautiful face, the face he had loved so much since childhood. "Bridget," he said, "you don't have to be. I'll wait until you are."

She smiled, shakily, and kissed him. It was only a peck, it was only on the cheek. But in that moment, they both knew that even that small kiss would provide enough comfort for the rest of their days.

HEAR MY LOVE

MICHELLE DAYE

Chapter 1

Violet reached for the knob on her stereo and turned the volume all the way up. If she listened very closely through the cloud of silence in her head, she could hear the low thrumming of the cello. The violins were gone. She should be hearing harp, too. Most people who lost their hearing lost the high notes first, and it was no different for her. All she could hear of the London Philharmonic Orchestra was bass and buzzing where once there was Handel's *Rejoicing*.

Angry tears stung her eyes, but she blinked them away. Nancy would be here any minute. Violet didn't want to be crying over her MP3 player when her friend got here.

Even as she thought Nancy's name, a hand landed on her shoulder. Violet yelped and turned, heart thumping. Vertigo gripped her, spinning through her head and swooping through her stomach. She might have fallen if not for the hand that caught her elbow. When her gaze finally steadied, it was Nancy's warm brown eyes and soft face that she saw.

Sorry, Nancy mouthed. Violet's best friend always kept her sentences short these days. She pulled a pained face, and added, *Too loud.*

Violet nodded apologetically and turned back, slowly this time, to click off the stereo. "I'm sorry," she said, and wondered how loud her voice must sound to Nancy if she could hear it herself. Just to be safe, she lowered her volume. "You know how people always ask each other what piece of music they'd choose if they could only hear one more? That was mine."

Nancy's mouth turned down, pitying. *Not the last*, she mouthed. *Have faith.* She pointed upward.

Violet nodded, but she didn't answer. She didn't have much to say to God lately. Ever since she was a child, she'd always believed He was the Great Physician, that He could heal anything if He wanted to. But He had not restored her hearing, no matter how hard she'd prayed.

How could He allow this to happen when He knew how much music meant to her? He had healed millions of people over the course of human existence, but He would not heal Violet.

Nancy reached for Violet's elbow again, and Violet allowed herself to be led forward through her living room. Her head swooped and spun with every step, and her stomach threatened to spill its contents all over her brightly-colored rug and shiny baby grand. She swallowed hard. *Not again,* she thought. Her nausea gradually faded as Nancy led her through her front door.

It was a sunny spring day, with a gem-blue sky overhead and a slight breeze to cool Violet's hot face. The cherry tree in her front yard had, in the last few days since she had dared to venture outside, burst into vibrant flower. Nancy's freshly washed car shone from the driveway where she'd parked. It was a beautiful day. Only Violet's mood was ugly.

Nancy opened the passenger-side door to her car and helped Violet inside.

"And they said chivalry was dead." Violet grinned.

Nancy smiled back, and the edges of her eyes crinkled. *Watch your feet,* she mouthed, shutting the door.

On the way to the hospital, Violet turned her attention to the yards and gardens of the houses they passed. All the grass had turned emerald green, and flowers bloomed riotously from gardens and cracks in sidewalks. *Spring,* she thought, and tried to bring Vivaldi to her mind. The strains of the piece still came easily to her memory, but she'd once been told auditory memories were among the soonest to fade. How long would she have this silent music to draw on for strength in hard times?

Someday, maybe she wouldn't remember what music sounded like at all.

Dr. Minelli's office was on the fourth floor of the hospital, so Nancy helped Violet onto the elevator and steadied her when the upward lurch made Violet fall against the mirrored wall.

Somehow, they made it into the audiologist's waiting room and checked in despite the return of Violet's nausea. It was a restful sort of room, with light blue walls and potted ferns on the tables beside the outdated magazines. A huge aquarium covered one wall, and Violet watched the fish dart back and forth between the glass walls of their home.

Nancy touched her shoulder when the nurse called for her, and together they followed the scrub-wearing man down the hall to a room with drawings of the inner ear on all the walls. Violet sat up on the paper-covered table and Nancy sat in a plastic chair against a wall.

Dr. Minelli wasn't Violet's normal doctor, but they'd met a few times when the pretty, dark-haired audiologist had consulted with old Dr. Farnam. Meniere's disease wasn't uncommon, but it wasn't something Violet's primary had spent a lot of time with, either. Nobody knew what caused the disease. Researchers blamed everything from allergies to autoimmune disorders.

Whatever caused it, the fact remained that Violet had a severe case. Slight vertigo and tinnitus had, over the course of years, degenerated to 90% deafness and vertigo so severe Violet had almost become an invalid. They had tried drugs to reduce fluid in her body, as well as drugs to keep her from becoming too stressed out; they'd given her pills for nausea and more months of physical therapy than she could even count anymore. But none of it had worked. At only twenty-seven years old, Violet was barely able to care for herself. She couldn't drive. She couldn't stand for any length of time. She couldn't even walk down a hallway without supporting herself against a wall.

Medically, they'd come to the last resort. If Violet wanted any hope of a normal life, if she wanted to be able to run in the park again or walk any potential children in a stroller, she had to have this surgery. Not that she'd have much chance for marriage and children without the ability to hear. What husband would have her now? Brian certainly wouldn't be interested in a woman who couldn't even hear him.

When Dr. Minelli finally came into the room, she gave Violet a huge smile and spoke to her in slow, clearly enunciated words. Violet couldn't hear conversational voice levels anymore, but she carefully watched the doctor's lips for information: *remove the labyrinth*, she managed to catch, though it was followed by gibberish. *Permanent deafness. Thursday the twenty-first.*

When Violet finally started to cry, Dr. Minelli's pretty face turned pitying and she placed a hand on Violet's shoulder. *We wouldn't do this unless it was absolutely necessary,* the doctor mouthed. *I'm so sorry.*

"What am I going to do?" Violet sobbed. "I'm a musician! How am I going to live? How am I going to communicate? I can hardly even read lips!"

Dr. Minelli sighed, and though Violet couldn't hear a noise as soft as a breath anymore, she saw the doctor's shoulders heave. She stood up and walked to the sparkling clean counter beside the sink where she'd washed her hands and brought back a pamphlet made of a folded computer print-out. She handed it to Violet, who grasped it as if taking a life preserver.

American Sign Language Classes, it said. A group of smiling people adorned the front cover. If any of them were deaf, Violet couldn't figure out why they looked so happy.

*

Nancy helped Violet into the car and walked around to the driver's side. The day was still beautiful, though the sun had risen enough to heat the inside of the car. Nancy turned on the air conditioner, and it struggled against the late spring weather to keep them cool. Violet watched the scenery roll by until they turned down a road leading away from her house. She shot Nancy a confused look.

"Hey, sis, my house is that way." Violet pointed in the other direction.

Nancy glanced at her passenger. Maybe Violet imagined the sly, slightly guilty look on her face. Then she looked back at the road and said something Violet couldn't translate.

"You have to look at me when you talk or I can't understand you, Nance," Violet said.

They rolled up to a stop sign. Nancy turned her face toward Violet and mouthed, *Going to church. Left my purse.*

Violet groaned. "I'll sit in the car, if that's okay with you. I really don't want a ton of well- meaning people falling over themselves to try to talk to me."

Nancy shook her head. *Pastor wants to see you about insurance*, she said. *You better come in.*

Heavy dread settled in Violet's belly. She couldn't possibly face the pastor, not today. He'd been text-messaging her for the better part of a month, ever since she found out she was going to have to have the labyrinthectomy. He'd been hoping she could return to work on the worship team soon. She'd been ignoring him because she didn't have the heart to tell him she never would. Nancy had told him, of course. It hadn't stopped his texted thoughtfulness.

She couldn't really afford to have her insurance cancelled now, though. The time for ignoring her boss was over.

They pulled into the church's familiar parking lot. Violet waited for her friend to come around and help her out of the car. Even if she was able to stand on her own, she might have stayed where she was until Nancy dragged her out.

The pastor wasn't the only one who'd been texting her. Brian had, as well. If God was listening to her, she'd pray for Brian to be anywhere but here. Of course, God wasn't listening. Not to her. Not today.

She knew he was present as soon as she walked through the church door. She could feel the pulsing of bass guitar through the soles of her flats, which meant he was here, practicing with the rest of the worship team. Practicing without her. Violet trained her eyes on the floor and let Nancy lead her past the nave and down the hall to the pastor's office. She willed Brian not to notice her and not to come out. She thought she'd made it home free when someone touched her elbow.

She looked up into a pair of jade-green eyes. Her heart sped up even as she willed it not to. Brian was as handsome as ever, with his straight, white smile and blond hair brushing his collar. He wasn't wearing his leather motorcycle jacket, which meant he'd draped it over the back of a chair somewhere. Violet made an attempt to return his happy smile, but she knew her own expression was tired and wan.

Hey, he mouthed, and then something garbled. She remembered the sound of his voice, raised in harmony with her own in praise to Almighty God. Now she couldn't even understand what he was saying. Violet frowned, and Brian's face fell. She immediately missed that smile. He lit her up with it. But telling him that would make sure he never left her alone.

"I can't understand you," she said instead. It was true in so many ways. Why did he keep trying to talk to her when he knew she couldn't hear him anymore? Why did he keep trying to convince her to go out with him when she'd made it so very clear that she couldn't?

Brian took a deep breath as if gathering himself. Slowly, carefully, he mouthed, *Did you get my texts?*

She sighed. And what was she supposed to say to that direct a question? Of course she'd gotten them. Her phone worked fine. It was her ears that were messed up.

"I've been busy," she said. "I'm having surgery later this month."

Brian's eyes turned sad, and he reached out to touch her arm again. *I'm so sorry.*

Was that the theme for today? Everybody was so very, very sorry. But none of them had to choose between the ability to walk and the ability to hear. Violet bit her tongue and didn't say that out loud. It wasn't Brian's fault she had this disease.

A finger tapped her arm, and she looked back at Nancy. Nancy gave Brian a twinkling smile. Violet was about to ask what that particular expression was supposed to mean when Nancy mouthed, *Go sit down. I'll bring pastor to you.*

Brian gave Nancy a grateful smile and offered Violet his arm. Oh, *that's* what they were up to. Nancy was trying to play matchmaker again. Violet scowled at her friend and pointedly did not reach for Brian.

"I can walk, thank you," Violet snapped. "I don't need to sit down."

Oh, come on. Brian made a broad gesture with his hands, echoing his mouthed words. *Take a load off.* He smiled again, this time even more charming than before. Nancy gave Violet a little shove, and she suddenly found that she had to take Brian's arm or rely on her own dizzy feet.

He smelled so nice. He always did. She turned to scowl at Nancy, who only smiled and waved. The traitor.

Brian led her to the nave and down to the front row. Her former bandmates stood on the stage behind the pulpit, dressed in casual clothes instead of their Sunday finery. Lisa, the lead singer, grinned and waved as Brian helped Violet take a seat. Randy, lead guitar, set down his instrument and jogged down the stairs. He leaned down gingerly to wrap Violet in a hug. His beard tickled her cheek, but his smile was bright and welcome.

Hey, girl, he mouthed. *Come to watch the auditions?*

"What auditions?" Violet looked up at Brian, who was scowling at Randy. Randy's smile became a chagrined grimace almost instantly and he said something to Brian that Violet couldn't catch.

Brian sighed and Randy moved aside. Brian crouched in front of her chair and mouthed, *Don't freak out.*

"Freak out?" Her stomach felt as if it had suddenly filled with lead and was about to tip over. "Why would I freak out? What's he talking about, auditions?" It clicked all at once. "Oh. I see. You're auditioning a new keyboard player."

Regret turned Brian's mouth down, and she knew she'd guessed correctly. They were filling her old job. They'd been down a keyboard player ever since Violet had been out of work. Of course they needed to fill her spot.

It all made sense to her logical mind. So why did she suddenly want to cry?

She pushed up out of her chair, trying to ignore the spinning in her head. Brian reached out to steady her, but she shrugged his hand away.

"I probably should get out of your way so you can work. I'm sure none of the keyboard players want to audition with your old bandmate watching." She gave Lisa a wave and smiled shakily at Randy. Randy smiled back, but he looked kind of sick and green.

Just once, Lord, she thought. *Just once, let me walk out of here with my dignity intact.* She took a careful step past Brian and pretended she didn't see him reaching protectively after her. Another step, and she was still on her feet. Could she dare to hope that God was actually listening to her for once?

Her head started to spin four steps in. She told herself to ignore it, but after another step she had to steady herself against a pew. She took another step.

It felt like something huge, maybe a giant, was pressing down on the top of her head. Despair flooded her in the split second before she crashed onto the ground.

Violet managed to get her hands between her face and the floor, so she only scraped her palms and bruised her pride. Hot tears stung her eyes. For a long moment, all she could do was kneel on the ground with her head spinning and try not to cry and vomit simultaneously.

It was probably thirty seconds before strong arms lifted her up and held her steady. She found herself pressed against Brian's hard chest and so ashamed she couldn't stand to look into his eyes. He tried to catch her gaze by moving into her line of sight, but Violet looked stubbornly away.

Another set of hands gripped her arm, and she turned to find Nancy beside her, looking regretful and anxious. Violet let her friend lead her away. Her cheeks still burned with shame as Nancy helped her into the car.

They didn't speak at all until they got to Violet's house. Violet wanted to fling open the door and storm inside, but she didn't want to end up sprawled out in her driveway with her neighbors gawking. So she waited for Nancy to come around and help her, even though Nancy was the last person on Earth she wanted to interact with.

Nancy's broad, dark face was mournful. *I'm so sorry,* she mouthed. Violet only scowled. Nancy didn't speak again until Violet was safely ensconced in the floral print easy chair that sat across from her couch.

"Why did you take me in there?" Violet demanded. "I didn't even get a chance to see the pastor! Did he really ask to see me?"

Nancy flushed so deeply that Violet knew he hadn't. *Brian asked to see you*, she mouthed. *He said he misses you.*

"He *misses* me! Nancy, I've told you a hundred times that I can't focus on dating right now. I can't understand a word he says. How am I supposed to carry on a relationship with a man I can't even hear?"

Nancy's jawline firmed up, and her dark eyes flashed. *You say that about everything. 'How am I supposed to do anything when I can't even hear?' You've stopped living. I never thought you were the type to roll over and die, but I guess I was wrong.*

Violet was so stunned she couldn't reply.

Brian cares about you, Nancy continued. *He always has. He doesn't care if you're deaf, or if you can play the piano anymore. He cares about you as a person.* She paused, and her angry face softened. *You're the only one who cares about that stuff, Vi. The rest of us just want you to be happy again. There was a time when Brian made you happy.*

"Do you know what made me happy?" Violet demanded. "Making music with the worship team made me happy. But I can't do that anymore, can I? And thanks to you, I am fully aware that they're replacing me!"

Nancy's eyes narrowed. Violet let her gaze follow Nancy all the way to the door as she waited for a response, but instead Nancy left the room and slammed the door behind her.

*

Around the house, when she was alone, Violet used a walker to get from place to place. She didn't always need it, but it kept her from falling down when the vertigo hit. It reminded her of when her grandmother used to toddle around her nursing home. Violet couldn't bring herself to add tennis balls to the feet. Just using the walker made her feel a hundred years old.

She decided on a salad for dinner, and shuffled around her kitchen with her walker, thinking more about what Nancy had said to her than about the tomatoes she was trying to cut. *I never thought you were the type to roll over and die.* Well, Nancy could just stick that in her pipe and smoke it. She was a little down right now (okay, maybe she was a lot down) but that didn't mean Violet had given up on life.

Did it?

She thought of Brian again, almost involuntarily. Their first date had been Chinese food and a long walk in the park. They'd talked and laughed like old friends all through dinner. As they'd walked together afterward, Brian had pointed out a cloud of fireflies and how they reflected in the rippling lake under the bridge. He'd reached for her hand then, and Violet had wished he'd never let go.

But that was before this last attack of her disease had finally damaged her ear canals so badly it couldn't be reversed. She would never hear Brian's soft, joyful laugh again. She would never again listen as he tuned his bass before a practice.

What musician would want to carry on a relationship with a deaf girl?

Sure, he kept texting her. Sure, he smiled at her and tried to talk to her when they met at the church. But that was probably because he felt obligated to. What kind of a jerk would stop seeing a girl because she went deaf?

Not a guy like Brian, that's for sure. So she'd made the hard decision for them both.

A hand landed on Violet's shoulder, and she felt herself shriek, even though she couldn't hear the sound she made. She turned so quickly she almost fell for the second time in one day, but strong hands caught her and held her up until her dizziness passed.

Nancy. Violet set her jaw and wondered if she should be angry that her friend was back again or if she should just hurry up and forgive her. Nancy had meant well, after all, even though she had been sneaky about it.

Violet decided on noncommittally sullen. "What do you want?"

Nancy held up a folded piece of paper for Violet to see. It was the same pamphlet Dr. Minelli had handed her earlier.

Let's go, Nancy mouthed.

Violet scowled. "Where? I'm trying to fix dinner right now."

Sign-language classes, Nancy said. *You need them. So do I.*

"Why do you need them?" Violet asked.

Nancy's dark eyes filled with tears. She blinked several times, probably to clear them. Violet's angry heart softened. *So I can talk to my best friend when she can't hear me anymore.*

Violet left her ingredients on the counter and took Nancy's arm to go outside. Nancy had left her car running and the passenger door open despite the late hour. That was just like her friend, to trust too much. If someone had stolen it, Nancy would say, *I guess they needed it more than I did.*

Violet had to smile. "You're lucky I live in a nice neighborhood."

Thanks to the headlights, it wasn't too dark to see Nancy's eyes roll.

*

The community college consisted of low buildings sprawled across a city block. The grounds were perfectly manicured expanses of lawn dotted with fountains and crisscrossed with broad paths. Even at this hour, it was lit up bright as day. Few people were around. Only the security guards in their motorized carts were visible. A youngish guard in the passenger seat waved and smiled. Nancy waved back, though Violet didn't.

Nancy picked a parking spot and led Violet into the nearest building. Inside, too, was brightly lit, and a group of people stood around in a lobby, talking and laughing. Violet's first instinct was to fall back away from them so they wouldn't try to talk to her. But on the edge, close to a classroom, a trio of young people signed excitedly to one another.

Violet stopped in her tracks. The brochure was right. Some of these happy people were deaf, too.

Their professor arrived a few minutes later. She was frazzled and wore glasses that were too big for her face, but she wrote her name on the chalk board with confident strokes. Dr. Porter, the board proclaimed. All of the chairs faced forward, so Dr. Porter could be clearly seen. Nancy and Violet took adjoining seats at the middle of the room and got down to business.

After class, while everyone was packing up their books and laptops, Dr. Porter wended her way through the desks to Violet and Nancy. She waved and gave them a friendly smile. As she introduced herself and welcomed them to the class, she mouthed all of her words clearly and signed as she spoke.

Tell me, Violet, she said, *how do you come to be learning ASL so late in life?*

Violet turned to Nancy, who gave her a supportive nod.

"I have Meniere's Disease," Violet said. "It effects the inner ear, so not only has my hearing been damaged past repair, but I also have vertigo and trouble with my balance. My doctor told me that the labyrinths in my ears have to be removed if I want to be able to walk again. She also gave me the brochure for this class. I wasn't going to come, but—" Violet shrugged—"Nancy insisted."

Dr. Porter smiled. *I'm so glad she did. For me, learning ASL was the turning point of my life. Before, I was shy and had trouble connecting with people. Now*—Dr. Porter paused to laugh—*it's impossible to shut me up. So to speak.*

Violet nodded. She wanted to laugh with the professor, but she just couldn't. Not today. "So you learned ASL later in life as well?"

Dr. Porter's fluent fingers continued to fly as she mouthed, *Yes. I lost my hearing in an accident about fifteen years ago. I spent roughly a year struggling through relationships in which I couldn't communicate. But then one day I decided I'd spent enough time feeling sorry for myself. I needed to be the change I wanted to see, as they say.*

"I admire your bravery," Violet told her. "I'm not sure if I'll ever get to the point where I'll be happy again. I'm a pianist and a singer, and I found out today that I'll never hear another piece of music, let alone perform one."

Dr. Porter reached out to place a comforting hand on Violet's shoulder. She had to break the touch before she could go on. *This is very fresh for you, and I can't blame you for being unsure how you'll go on. But if I may offer some unsolicited advice, I'd like to remind you that Beethoven was deaf toward the end of his life.*

"Right," Violet agreed. "He composed Ode to Joy when he could no longer hear the orchestra. But I'm not a genius. I'm just a worship leader at my church."

Dr. Porter smiled, gently and sadly. *It's not his ability to compose without his hearing that I'd like you to emulate. It's his refusal to give up.*

Like you said, he wrote Ode to Joy while he was deaf. That isn't a piece of music composed by a man who has forgotten that life is worth living.

Violet found that she couldn't respond. She was suddenly overcome by shame. *Oh, Lord,* she thought. *I've forgotten how beautiful life can be, haven't I? I've forgotten to be grateful.*

Dr. Porter patted Violet's shoulder again. *I hope to see you Wednesday, Violet.*

"You will," Violet said, and she meant it.

*

ASL class was on Monday and Wednesday, and Nancy picked Violet up for it every time. They sat together and practiced together, signing slowly and clearly to help each other pick it up. It was a small step, and learning a new language was difficult, but the class made Violet feel hopeful for the first time since she'd found out she might lose her hearing. Maybe she'd have to learn a new career, but at least she had friends who cared enough to break through the silence.

The day before her surgery, Nancy offered to stay home and eat ice cream with Violet instead of going to class, but Violet decided to go anyway. She wanted the moral support of friendly classmates and her understanding professor. She didn't expect to see a giant bouquet of spring flowers with a card signed by everyone in her ASL class.

She found that evening that she could still sign with tears in her eyes: *Thank you all. This means so much to me.*

She and Nancy carried the flowers out after class, and Violet fervently prayed that she wouldn't drop them and break the vase. When Nancy stopped short, she almost toppled over.

Don't look now, Nancy signed, *but we have company.*

Violet followed Nancy's gaze. Brian sat at one of the tables in the lobby, eating a sandwich and studying a textbook. He still wore his leather jacket despite the warmth of the room. A pair of wire-rimmed reading glasses Violet had never seen before perched delicately on the bridge of his nose. Her heart clenched hard. Even in glasses, looking out of place in this tweedy setting, he was still gorgeous. She had almost managed to stop missing him until right now.

He's taking classes here? Violet signed. *What for?*

Nancy shrugged. *Should we talk to him, or just keep walking?*

She thought of the last time she'd seen him, when she'd pitched head-over-heels and he'd had to pick her up. Violet's cheeks burned with embarrassment.

Keep walking, Violet signed. She lifted the flowers up to cover her still-red face and they left through the opposite door.

*

The surgery went exactly as it was supposed to, and Violet woke up inside a shroud of silence thick as a building's foundation. She'd been prepared for it, but it still hit her hard enough to knock her into bed for a week. Nancy came every day to make sure Violet was eating and to bring her the homework from their class. She signed to Nancy that her head hurt (it did) to make sure Nancy let her stay in bed, but of all her post-surgery aches, it was her heart that hurt the worst.

It was seven o'clock on Tuesday evening when she woke up from a pain-pill induced sleep to the strains of Bach playing through her head. She lay in bed in the early evening gloom, staring at the ceiling. There was a time, not long ago, when she could play that song from memory. Could she still do it? The keys would feel the same, even if she couldn't hear them.

Violet lifted herself slowly out of bed, but the dizziness didn't hit her as immediately as usual. In fact, as she re-gained her feet, she realized she could stand without her feet slipping out from under her.

She made her way into the living room and sat down on the piano bench. She positioned her hands in the old, familiar way and began to play. She couldn't hear a note of it. But the muscle memory was still there, and if she thought of it, she could remember the sound of this piece she loved so much.

It wasn't much, but it was something. Her music wasn't gone. It was just different.

A hand landed on her shoulder and she shrieked. Behind her, Brian stood with his hands in the air to show their emptiness.

I'm sorry, he mouthed, while her heart still pounded against her ribcage. Then he brought his hands together and signed, *I'm sorry. I'm sorry I startled you. I texted you that I was coming over, but you didn't respond.*

For a moment, she was too stunned to do anything but hold her hands against her chest. What was he doing here? Had Nancy forgotten to lock the door when she left this afternoon? Oh, Lord, how did her hair look? She hadn't taken a shower in two days.

But the question she asked was, *When did you learn how to sign?*

Brian flushed with embarrassment and he signed back, *I've been taking a class at the community college. It seems like some of the people I like the best can't hear very well these days.*

Did he—did he mean her? Violet stood. Brian reached out to steady her, but she was firm on her feet. She gestured to her couch and signed, *Won't you sit down?*

Brian gave her that familiar, beautiful smile and did as she directed. She joined him there on the cushion.

You sound great, he signed. *Just as nice as ever.*

Violet shrugged. *It's strange not to be able to hear my own playing.*

Brian's smile faded. *I can imagine. Hey, I brought you something, but I left it in my car. I'll be right back.*

She waited for him to return, watching the door so he wouldn't have to touch her shoulder again. He re-appeared a few moments later with a box, which he placed beside her on the couch.

It's a door light, he signed. *Nancy said that you can't hear the doorbell and that she often startles you when she comes to visit. I found this online and*—he shrugged. *It seems like a really easy way to solve a problem.*

She wasn't sure how to process all of this. *How thoughtful,* she signed. *I don't know what to say.*

Brian grinned again. *I'll set it up. Just give me a second.*

He bustled around her house, from door to computer to back again. She had never realized, when she could hear his voice, how gracefully he moved. Had he studied dance? And how had she managed to work with him for an entire year without noticing how those long hands were good for more than teasing out a bassline?

When he was finished, he placed a white square of plastic on her piano and gestured for her to stay still. He ran around to the front door again, and suddenly the thing flashed a pulsing light.

Brian came back in smiling. Violet smiled back and signed, *It works great! Thank you!*

It's so great to see you smiling, Brian signed. *Last time you smiled at me like this was when I held your hand that night at the park. Do you remember that? We were walking over the bridge, looking at the fireflies.*

I remember, Violet signed. Oh, why had she let him stay? She knew what he felt for her, and she'd let him into her life again anyway. What did it matter if she felt the same way? She could never have a real relationship with Brian when she knew how important music was to him. Hesitantly, she signed, *Brian, look.*

He held up a hand to stop her. *Don't worry. You told me you don't have space in your life for a romantic relationship. I totally understand that. But I care about you, Violet. I just want to be in your life in whatever way you'll let me. If that's just as your friend, then that's what I'll be.*

Her heart swelled. Why, oh why did he have to be so good? If he was some pushy jerk who just wanted his own way, she would throw him out of her house and never set eyes on him again. But this? How could she turn away the friendship of so good a man?

It's not that I don't care about you. It's just that it would never work out with us. How could somebody with your musical talent be with a deaf girl? It just doesn't make sense.

Brian reached out and took both of her hands in his. Very slowly, very clearly, he mouthed, *None of that matters to me, Violet. Whether you can hear me or not, you understand what's in my heart. And I understand what's in yours. Most people who can hear each other don't have that much going for them.*

"Brian, I—" she could feel the words in her mouth, but she couldn't hear them at all. She gave up. What was the point?

He let go of her hands and stood up. *Like I said,* he signed, *I'm your friend. Hey, if you feel up to it, you should come to service on Sunday. The band and I have a surprise for you.*

I'll see what I can do, Violet signed. She walked Brian to the door and shut it behind him.

*

Saturday night, Violet couldn't sleep. She tossed and turned in her bed, watching the shadows change on her ceiling. *The band has a surprise for me,* she thought. *Randy and Lisa and whoever it is they picked to replace me.* Brian too, of course. Brian, who understood what was in her heart. Who was convinced she understood what was in his. Brian, who said he wanted to be her friend but smiled at her in a way that made her feel like the only woman on earth. Brian, who had learned to sign when she could no longer hear his voice.

There would be other people there, too. There would be people she had known for years but would no longer be able to speak to. There would be people who would want to know why she hadn't showed her face in church for such a long time. What would she say to them? *Well, I'm deaf now. I can't hear the sermon.* Or maybe even, *God has forgotten me, so now I'm busy forgetting him.* What was old Mrs. Jenkins going to say to that? She would definitely not look kindly on a crisis of faith from a person who'd been a worship leader. Nobody understood what it was like for her to be cut off from music. It was like she'd died.

Why, Lord? She thought. *Why did You let this happen to me? Why would You give me this musical ability and then take it away?*

A still, small voice inside of her answered, *Sometimes, you can't see what's really important until you clear out what isn't.*

As those words ran through her head like a mantra, Violet was finally able to fall asleep.

She woke the next morning without benefit of an alarm clock and took her shower. Violet chose her clothes carefully, curled her hair, and applied her make-up with a steady hand.

Well, she couldn't hear, but she sure looked good.

She hadn't yet fixed her car up with the interior signals she would need to drive, so Nancy picked her up. She grinned hugely and threw her arms around Violet in a tight hug.

The church parking lot was full of shiny cars and happy people wearing their best clothes. When she got out of the car, Mr. Hernandez hurried over. He spoke quickly, and Violet frowned. Nancy stopped him with a touch on his arm, and Mr. Hernandez stopped talking, turned to face Violet directly, and mouthed, *It's so good to see you, Violet. We've all really missed you.*

As she made her way inside, it seemed as if everyone had missed her. She found that she'd really missed them, too. All this time that she'd been holed up in her house, leaving it only for doctor's appointments and ASL classes, she hadn't realized how thin and attenuated her spirit had become. But when these people hugged her, they fed her soul. She felt lifted, and fulfilled, and very, very loved.

Pastor found her in the lobby before she sat down. *Violet!* He mouthed. *I'm so glad to see you! Can you stick around after the service to talk? I have an idea about how we can keep you on your insurance.*

That would be amazing, Violet replied.

Brian, Lisa, and Randy weren't around, but she wasn't surprised. They would be backstage, preparing their music and warming up their voices. They might even be prepping the new keyboard player, depending how long they'd been together. She sat with Nancy in the front row of the nave where it would be easy to read Pastor's lips when he talked. What she didn't catch, Nancy translated into sign for her.

Nancy had to translate, *I'd like to welcome our worship team to the stage now. They have a very special presentation they've prepared for a member of our congregation. Let's hear it!*

A blaze of light kicked on, bright white as the sun, and the band swaggered out onto the stage. Lisa waved and picked up her microphone. Randy followed her, then a woman Violet didn't know who took up residence behind the keyboard, and finally, Brian sauntered out in his leather jacket, grinning. He waved at Violet, who waved back. Her stomach flipped twice. It was almost ridiculous how good-looking he was.

The lights strobed yellow, then green, like the footlights in a rock show. Instead of holding up his bass, Brian took a section of stage next to Lisa. When Randy started to strum and Lisa took up her mic, Brian signed, *This is for you, Violet. You don't have to listen to understand my heart.*

Nancy shot her a sly, sideways smile, but Violet couldn't take the time to pay attention to her. The lights at the bottom of the stage weren't the only ones—the ceiling had been strung with fairy lights, and these flashed in rhythm, changing colors and sparkling against the dimmed lights of the nave. Lisa raised her mic to her lips and began to sing. Beside her, Brian signed the words to a worship song they had sung together a thousand times. In her memory, the sound of his sweet baritone spiraling with her own toward heaven was so strong she could almost hear it. She could feel the presence of God Almighty more strongly than she had in months. Tears stung her eyes and raced down her cheeks. *Sometimes, you can't see what's really important until you clear out the rest.*

*

After the service, Brian found Violet in the lobby. Nancy squeezed her hand and moved away to talk to someone else, leaving her alone with the handsome bass player.

What did you think? Brian signed.

Violet had been wondering what she would say to him ever since his set ended. There had been so many things racing through her mind then. But now, in this moment, all she could manage was, *I don't think anyone has ever done something like this for me. It was so beautiful.*

Brian smiled. *I got the idea from the doorbell I brought you. I thought, she may not be able to hear anymore, but that isn't the only way to experience music.*

Violet wrapped her arms around his shoulders and went up on her tiptoes. She kissed his mouth very softly, like a promise. Brian slid his arms around her waist and held her against him. He said nothing. He didn't need to.

Someone tapped her shoulder, and Violet turned. Pastor stood behind her, smiling knowingly. Brian let her go so suddenly she almost stumbled, but she caught herself on his shoulder before she could.

Pastor said, *I was thinking, your insurance won't be cancelled if you still work here. The church sure could bring in a lot more parishioners if we had a full-time ASL translator.*

For the second time that Sunday morning, tears filled Violet's eyes. *I hear You, Lord,* she thought. *I hear You loud and clear.*

ACTING AMISH

MONICA MARKS

Acting Amish

"Fie, fie! Unknit that threatening unkind brow and dart not scornful glances from those eyes..."

Alessandra's stormy dark eyes stared out at her wedding audience, embarking on her monologue as her peripheral vision nervously surveyed the little she could see of the real audience. The stage lights were too bright for her to see much beyond the first and second rows.

Is he out there? Is he watching me right now?

The last letter he had sent was particularly unnerving and Dennis had told her to call off the performance.

"I'm Kate," she snapped at her agent, applying mascara to her already long lashes. "I can't just not show to a performance."

"You do have an understudy," Dennis replied dryly.

"The people are not here to watch Samantha screw up lines. I have seen buskers do better Shakespeare than her."

Dennis rolled his eyes but turned serious at the true subject matter.

"Alex, did you read what he – "

"I have eyes, Dennis and yes, I am able to read, thank you." She wished he would go away. She wanted some time to meditate before curtain call and Dennis was blocking her chakra.

"Alex – "

"Listen, I don't pay you to give me advice," she told him coldly, spinning in her chair to stare at him. "That is what I pay my life coach for."

Dennis' lips pursed into a fine line of defiance.

"You're being foolish," he told her. "But I suppose it wouldn't be the first time. It may, however, be the last time. No need for a life coach if you're dead, is there?"

His last sentence sent chills down her spine but Alessandra did not show her fear. She was a classically trained actress, after all.

"Are you sure you don't act? Your flair for melodrama is fantastic!"

Dennis narrowed his wrinkled eyes and stormed from the dressing room, leaving Alessandra to return to her reflection.

Staring back at her was a surprisingly beautiful face with a glow of innocence. Her widely spaced brown eyes portrayed earnestness and a mass of auburn hair spilled becomingly around her high cheekbones. It was a face that had captured the off-Broadway crowd for years, her toes ever touching the line of the bigtime.

I must be doing something right; I have a stalker, she thought wickedly but she was instantly ashamed at her tactless thought. It was hardly a joking matter but if she did not put a twisted spin on the danger she was facing, she feared she would lose her mind.

"...my hand is ready; may it do him ease."

She finished her soliloquy and turned, allowing the other players to speak their piece but she could not stop her gaze from shifting from Petruchio to the overflowing seats in the Open Stage of Harrisburg. It was her final night playing Katharina in Shakespeare's "Taming of the Shrew" at the regional theater and she was looking forward to the break before starting her role as Cosette in "Les Misérables" in the spring.

Thank God I will be on the West Coast for "Les Mis." I can't get out of here fast enough. It will be good riddance to Pennsylvania. I don't think I'll ever come back to this state, Alex told herself, trying to refocus her attention on the cast. *That lunatic has ruined the Keystone State for me forever.*

"Tis a wonder by your leave, she will be tamed so."

The scene was over and applause erupted deafeningly as the curtain fell.

Curtain calls and then we're done. Almost there, she tried to reassure herself but with each bow she took among her fellow actors, the more dread filled her stomach.

"If you do not act for me, you must not act at all!" the last in the series of letters had read.

"You must call the police!" Dennis had shouted but Alessandra had brushed him off, dismissing his concerns as trivial.

"Oh please! That is exactly what this whack job wants; attention. I flat out refuse to alter my life and cower in fear because of some weirdo who slips notes in obscure places."

Alex did not admit to Dennis that she constantly looked over her shoulder, staring at every man as if he was a potential threat. She was paranoid in the most casual of circumstances.

You are letting him get the best of you anyway, she told herself angrily. It was not like Alessandra to be so jumpy and yet she would be naïve not to recognize the danger of a crazed fan.

Red roses were thrown on stage and she received a standing ovation which she accepted graciously, flashing her award-winning smile to the adoring admirers, exhaling greatly when the curtain fell for the last time.

She hurried back to her dressing room, eager to leave the theater.

I am going back to the hotel, soaking in a bubble bath and having an entire bottle of champagne to myself, she vowed, taking off her wig and shaking out her reddish-brown tresses. She could not move fast enough it seemed but blessedly, she was grabbing her handbag and heading for the back exit before she could be coaxed into staying for the afterparty. Alex was not in the mood to see anyone else, not that night.

I'll bite the bullet and take those hams out for lunch before I leave Pennsylvania on the weekend, just in case I have the misfortune of having to work with them again.

She hoped not; the entire cast seemed a talentless hack embodied.

I'm going to have to find a better agent. Dennis keeps setting me up in these places where no critic will get to see me shine, not in the midst of people who can't accentuate my artistic flair. I can't carry the entire crew all the time.

She pushed her way into the bitter January night, the cold assaulting her lungs. A medium snow had begun to fall from the sky, dusting the cars in the parking lot indifferent and Alex cringed as she hurried toward her Mazda Miata. She hoped that there was not ice beneath the snow. Firing up the small vehicle, she reached into the back of the convertible for the scraper, grimacing.

Stupid Pennsylvania winter. I can't wait to get home to Florida where it only snows oranges.

Without gloves, she attacked the caking of white from her blood red car.

Suddenly, something slipped around her neck, yanking her backward. Alessandra's hand flew to her throat, shock shaking her body.

"Good evening, Alessandra," he rasped in her ear. "I am so happy to finally meet you. I'm sorry it has to be under these circumstances."

Dennis is right. I am going to die, she thought, closing her eyes. *And I was so close to fame...so close...I suppose being murdered will make me famous too...*

The snow was driving wickedly against the almost completely open area and Christian could barely see in front of his face. The wagon was making its way laboriously toward the district and he hoped they were not far. He had no way of knowing where he was with the storm so intense. He silently prayed that Ferd, his horse would make his way back safely.

Christian lowered his head, hoping to stave off some of the pelting ice but the action was futile at best.

You have been in worse storms, he tried to tell himself but instantly another voice demanded to know when. Optimism was not his strongest suit.

The storm had come in swiftly and without warning or Christian would have packed up his booth at the market hours earlier. In his haste to leave, he had abandoned some of his wares but a lot of good that had done; he was still trapped in the middle of the blizzard.

Suddenly Ferd snorted, pausing suspiciously and Christian raised his head to see what had spooked his horse.

Initially, he could not reconcile what it was at the side of the white blanketed road. Beneath the pile of white was a small mound of something but what?

He urged Ferd forward and stopped him beside the foreign object. Shifting down the bench of the wagon, reigns still in hand, Christian reached out to touch the snow-capped heap. To his surprise, it was a vehicle.

This is the smallest car I have ever seen, he thought, peering as best he could at it.

"Hello?" he called out into the wind. He saw no signs of life, no flashing hazards but he felt the need to make his voice heard, lest there be a body in the nearby snow. It was nearly impossible to see but they might hear his voice over the wind.

If someone has broken down here in this storm, it is a long way to travel for help, he thought with concern. Under normal circumstances, Christian would not have bothered to stop, knowing that someone else would be along the road. Yet he could not in good conscious leave whomever in the unforgiving storm. There was no telling when the skies might clear.

Ferd protested as Christian dismounted, poking around the car, wiping snow off windows to see inside. His blue eyes widened in shock when he saw a young woman slumped over the steering wheel, a mass of auburn hair covering her face.

"Oh *Gotte*," Christian muttered, searching for the handle to the door. He hoped he would not have to break the window to get her out and he prayed she was simply unconscious and not dead. To his relief, the driver's door gave way and he reached inside to feel for a pulse. He exhaled and silently thanked God. She was breathing.

"Miss?" he called at her but she did not respond. He tried to shake her but she was limp.

She likely slid off the road and hit her head. I do not see blood but she may have a head injury.

His heart racing, he slipped off his hand coverings and touched her. She was near frozen and Christian was suddenly terrified that she would die before he found help for her.

She might have hypothermia already or internal bleeding. Perhaps she had broken bones...

There were dozens of things which Christian could think of which could kill her before they arrived in safety.

He pulled her from the seat and fought against the wind to lay her inside the darkness of the wagon. Grabbing the blanket he had been using for himself, he wrapped her carefully and hurried back to the bench.

"Hurry Ferd," he told the horse, tapping the reins briskly. Suddenly he was no longer cold. He was only afraid for the pale, injured woman in his wagon.

"Good evening, Alessandra," he rasped in her ear. "I am so happy to finally meet you. I'm sorry it has to be under these circumstances."

Shock filled her body as the scarf tightened around her throat and Alessandra clawed at the fabric hysterically. Her eyes darted around, hoping for a witness, anyone who might chance into the back parking lot but she had purposely parked in the most secluded part of the area, hoping to slip away unnoticed.

"Shh, don't fight, my love," he purred. "You are an angel, I knew it when I first laid eyes on you and you will go to heaven where angels belong."

Unexpectedly, a shot of clarity sparked through Alessandra's panicked psyche and her eyes fell on the scraper resting on the hood of her car. She lunged forward, catching her attacker off guard, whirling to jam him in the face with the de-icer.

He screamed, grabbing at his face and Alessandra seized the opportunity to jump into her already running car, gasping for air. She had not caught her breath but she dared not stop, backing the convertible out of the snowy spot and spinning wildly from the parking lot.

He's coming for me! She thought, her eyes glued to the rear-view mirror but all she could see was a wall of white in her hindsight.

I have to get out of here. I don't care where I go but I can't stay here!

She steered the car precariously onto interstate 83 heading east, willing herself not to look back but she could not stop herself from expecting a set of headlights to run her off the road.

Just keep driving, she thought. *When you are sure you are not being followed, reach for your cell and call for help.*

She swallowed, thinking about what she would say to Dennis.

He is going to be so smug when he hears what happened, she realized with some annoyance. *I shouldn't call him. I will call the police.*

She reasoned that the result would be the same; in either case, she would be made a mockery of amongst her peers.

Why didn't I take this crazy person more seriously? She wondered, her mind in a thousand different places. *Who is this man and why is he so fixated on me?*

Alessandra reminded herself that she was very talented and quite easy on the eyes. It was hardly a shock that she would have many admirers but to want her dead?

If he kills me, how is he going to continue to watch me on stage? I don't understand any of this.

She was not paying attention, her car sliding through the black ice and the storm grew worse. At some point, Interstate 83 had become Route 322 but she had not noticed any signs.

All she knew was that she had been driving for well over an hour and the roads were becoming worse to handle with each passing mile.

He is not following me, Alessandra convinced herself, reaching her right hand toward her purse. She rifled through, feeling for her cell but the bag was deep and filled with unmentionable items.

Don't tell me I left it at the theater, she thought, her heart beginning to thud frantically. *It's okay, you just need to stop at a rest stop or something and make a phone call if you did.*

It was then she realized she had not seen a town in many miles.

Have I missed my last chance for gas or a telephone? What if I get stranded and he catches up with me? I will have nowhere to run and no cell to call for help.

Her hand became a flurry of desperation and she tore her eyes away from the blinding snow to look inside the purse. Immediately she located it, stuffed in an inside pocket. Exhaling, she pulled it out and unlocked it, scanning through her contacts.

The moment she pressed send, the car hit another patch of black ice on the isolated road and the Miata went careening out of control.

Alessandra's last thought before losing consciousness was that she had accidentally dialled Dominos Pizza and not Dennis.

"Who is she?" David asked, peering at the pale face in the single bed. She had not stirred since Christian had brought her home and he feared the worst.

"I do not know but I think she needs a doctor," Christian replied gravely. He was relieved that her skin seemed to have warmed some in the heat of the small farmhouse but her parlor was cause for concern.

"In this weather, who else can we call?" his neighbor asked, peering at his wife nervously and Christian recognized the truth in David's words. Until the snow let up, it would only endanger anyone sent to call on a doctor in the district. It had been a blessing that David and Elizabeth were nearby or else Christian would have been left to tend to the woman alone.

"Did she have anything with her? A bag or identification lest she perish in the night? We will not know whom to contact without it," David pressed and Christian sighed.

"I did not think to look. The weather was treacherous and I only wanted to find shelter and safety." David nodded understandingly and gestured for his wife to follow them from the room.

"I imagine if it comes to that, she has something in her vehicle," Christian offered but he sincerely hoped it would not reach such a dire end. There had been enough death in his home for many lifetimes.

"There is little else we can do for now," David told Christian. "We will return home as the hour is quite late but if you should need us, come calling."

Christian reluctantly walked them to the door, glancing into the night in hopes that the snow had let up but it showed no sign of slowing.

"I will," Christian replied, watching the couple return to lot across the snowy country road. He slowly closed the door in their absence and leaned against it, his mind racing. There was a familiar feeling to the scene, something he thought he had finally overcome but seeing the woman in the tiny car had resurfaced a series of very unpleasant memories.

It is as if I am watching Hannah dying all over again, he thought, the image of his younger sister weighing heavily on his mind.

She is not Hannah. She is an Englisher who will wake up healthy and unharmed, Christian told himself, forcing positivity into his thoughts. Yet as usual, the other voice, the grim, dark one responded.

Or she will not wake up and she will die just like everyone else who has lived in this house.

Christian forced the thought away and climbed to the second floor so he could be near the stranger should she wake.

There is something else I can do, he thought firmly. *I can pray.*

"O Romeo, Romeo, wherefore art thou Romeo? Deny thy father and refuse thy name – "Alessandra whirled to stare at Romeo but he was the crazed fan who had tried to take her life.

"Good evening, Alessandra. I am so happy to finally meet you. I'm sorry it has to be under these circumstances."

"That is not your line!" she screamed, turning to flee the stage but he grabbed her by the arm, wrapping a scarf around her wrist. *"You are reading the wrong lines!"*

"All angels belong in heaven," he recited, his brow furrowing in concentration, pulling her close so his hands could encircle her throat.

"No!" she shrieked, struggling to escape. *"That is not the line either! You're reading the wrong lines!"*

"Miss! Miss, it is but a bad dream!"

Her hands lashed out and contacted skin before her dark eyes opened. Alessandra stared blankly at the strange man, the effects of wakefulness clashing dramatically with the terror of her dream.

Is this the stalker? No, he doesn't look anything like the man who tried to kill me but where am I? How did I get here?

Slowly, her arms lowered as she remembered the drive from Harrisburg through Interstate 83 and losing control of the car.

"Are you well?" the man peered at her cautiously and Alessandra realized she was in a bed.

"Where am I?" she breathed, sitting up. Her head was swimming.

"You are in Lancaster County. I found you unconscious in a vehicle a few miles from here yesterday evening," he told her. "Earlier this night. It is four o'clock in the morning now."

There was something odd about the way he spoke as if he had an indiscernible accent but his English was perfect.

She blinked uncomprehendingly at him.

"Lancaster County?" she echoed. Why did she know Lancaster County?

"Are you injured somewhere?" he questioned, seemingly ill at ease and Alessandra wasn't sure how to respond. Instantly, her biting wit came into play.

"Oh no, I'm wonderful," she chirped sarcastically. The man stared quizzically at her with vivid blue eyes and Alex wondered if he was slow.

Or what if he's crazy too? What if I walked into another dangerous situation?

She was instantly reminded of a Stephen King movie and she shuddered, trying to sit up.

"I would rest," he suggested. "You have been through quite an ordeal. What is your name?"

She ignored his advice and swung her legs over the side of the small bed, relieved to find she was still dressed. In fact, she was wearing an extra sweater and too large pair of socks. Immediately, her head began to swim, black spots dancing in front of her eyes.

"What's your name?" she challenged back, unwilling to divulge information to a stranger. As far as she knew, he was a psychopath interested in harvesting her organs. She had seen that episode of 60 Minutes too.

"Christian Plank," he replied without hesitation but he continued to stare at her.

"Why are you looking at me like that?" she demanded, scouring the floor for her boots. She did not see them.

"Miss?"

"You're looking at me funny. Where are my shoes? I have to get out of here."

Christian chuckled mirthlessly.

"You are not going anywhere," he replied shortly as Alessandra rose. Dizziness knocked her back down the bed and she stared up at him, fear coloring her face.

"You can't keep me here," she declared with more conviction than she felt. Christian shook his head, a dry smile touching his lips but she could see it did not meet his eye.

"I have no interest in keeping you here, Miss," he assured her, stepping back as if to give her space. "But I fear we are in the midst of a terrible snowstorm."

Alessandra cocked her head to the side and glared at him.

"Last I heard, cars still run in snowstorms. Has anything changed since yesterday? Do we still have cars?"

Christian seemed angered by her tone and he snorted derisively.

"As I mentioned, I found you in your car which is miles from here," he replied shortly.

"Well drive me back to it," she snapped. This time when Christian laughed, it was genuine.

"Miss, you are in the middle of Amish country in a blizzard. Unless you would prefer to sleep in the barn, you are here until the weather clears."

Alessandra stared at him, her mouth agape.

"Amish country?" she repeated. It hit her then; *that* was where she recognized the name Lancaster County. But instead of dismay filling her body, she was overcome with a burst of relief.

He will never think to look for me in Amish county, she thought happily. *I can call the police and stay here until my stalker is caught!*

She smiled brilliantly at Christian, suddenly flopping back against the pillows.

"Perfect!" she said happily. "I'll stay here then."

Her savior seemed confused by her about face.

"Until the weather lets up," he told her. "You may stay until then."

Alessandra's smile widened and she winked at him conspiratorially.

"We'll see. You may like me so much, you won't want me to go."

I'm not going anywhere.

Christian studied her, his confusion apparent.

"Are you hungry? Can I offer you something to drink?"

"I suppose wine is out of the question, hm?"

Christian seemed to be losing his patience with her.

"There is no alcohol in this house," he answered tightly.

"Even Jesus drank wine," she replied coyly and Christian scowled at her openly. He pressed his lips together to refrain from answering sharply.

Something occurred to Alessandra who was oblivious to the way she was grating on her host's nerves.

"Where is my purse?" she asked, again looking around the room.

"I imagine it is in your vehicle. I did not bring anything from your auto but you," he told her. Alessandra glowered at him in disbelief.

"You left my purse in the car?" she screeched and he winced.

"My concern was not your belongings," he answered quietly. "If there is nothing you require, I am retiring for what is left of the night."

He was gone before Alessandra could protest, shutting the door firmly behind him. She looked around the simple room and turned her attention outside to the storm.

Whether it snows or not, I am not going anywhere. Not until there is word that my psycho stalker is tucked away behind some iron bars for a long while.

Christian could not sleep, his mind flooded with irritation and anger.

I should have known nothing good would come from picking up an Englisher but what choice did I have? I could not just leave her there. She is uncouth and disrespectful of the Amish way.

He tried to reason that she probably did not know much about his way of life but that did not excuse her bratty behavior.

She acts like a spoiled child. She did not even express gratitude for being rescued. I hope this storm clears soon so I will be rid of her.

For a moment, a fleeting image of Hannah crossed through her mind but it was gone as soon as it appeared.

Hannah was willful when she was not ill, he remembered and instantly he was struck with contrition for the thought.

That girl is nothing like my deceased sister.

It was at that moment he realized that he had not learned the woman's name.

"She woke then?" Elizabeth asked, brushing the snow off her cloak as she ducked inside Christian's house to avoid being dumped upon further. The storm was still raging in chips of ice and blustering winds.

Christian stifled a sigh and nodded.

"Yes, in the middle of the night," he answered.

"How wonderful," Eliza breathed happily. "How is she this morning? Does she need medical attention?"

Christian shook his head.

"She is unharmed and I have not seen her yet this morning. She is still asleep."

His neighbor blinked at the unexpected answer.

"It is nearing noon!" she cried but immediately she shook her head. "But of course, she must need the rest after all she has endured."

"Who is shrieking?"

The woman appeared at the top of the stairs, as if she was about to make a dramatic descent. Christian grudgingly admitted that she was lovely despite her dishevelled appearance.

"Good morning, Miss," Eliza called up to her. "I am Christian's neighbor, Elizabeth. How are you faring today?"

"Ugh," she groaned. "My head is pounding. I could use an Advil but I guess that's not going to happen."

Eliza glanced at Christian in surprise and then back up at her.

"We do not have medication but Christian does know the art of reflexology quite well. Perhaps he can ease your headache."

Christian groaned inwardly but before he could protest, the woman had glided down the stairs toward him.

"Really? You know reflexology?" she asked curiously. "Can you try?"

Christian gritted his teeth, tempted to refuse but Elizabeth was already smiling happily.

"I will be on my way. I only came to see how our guest was doing. Good day." She was gone before either one could utter a sound and Christian peered at the woman.

"Hands or feet?" she asked.

"Hands," he replied without any warmth. "Sit down."

She did obligingly, stripping off the extra sweater he had put on her the night before.

"I am so glad you have a bathroom in this place," Alessandra stated. "I think I would have demanded you bring me a pot if not."

Christian wrenched her hands from the table.

"Which side of your head hurts?"

"Both," she replied, rolling her neck. He paused and stared at the red marks he saw crisscrossed about her throat.

"What happened to you?" he asked quietly. Her dark eyes widened as she realized where he was staring and yanked her hands back, covering herself.

"Nothing," she replied sharply, her eyes darting about in a sudden panic.

Is that something she did to herself or did someone do that to her? Christian wondered, his heart hammering. Again, a picture of Hannah flittered through his mind and he tried to shove it away but he could not.

Did she try to do what Hannah did?

The woman cleared her throat.

"My headache is gone," she told him suddenly. "I'm going back to lay down."

He watched her disappear back into the hallway, a pang of melancholy jolting through him.

Is this woman Hannah coming back to me?

The snow began to slow by the mid afternoon and by early evening, it had finally stopped.

Alessandra stole down the stairs, peeking into the sitting room for Christian who had fallen asleep in front of the fire, reading the bible.

For a moment, she stood watching him, a strange sense of de ja vu washing through her as if she had been in that very spot, staring at the attractive man who had saved her life.

He really didn't have to stop for you. If he was anyone else, he would have left you to freeze to death. Did you ever thank him?

A flood of guilt threatened to drown her as she realized she had not.

Slowly, she stepped forward, putting her hand on his arm and shook gently.

"Christian," she whispered. He murmured slowly in his sleep and Alex leaned lower to hear the words he was speaking.

"Christian," she breathed again and suddenly his bright blue eyes flew open.

"What are you doing here?" he sputtered, sitting up and Alessandra stepped back.

"I'm sorry," she told him. "I wanted to thank you for everything you've done for me. I – I was running from a bad situation and it occurred to me that I wasn't very grateful to you."

Christian stared at her, his eyes registering surprise.

"You do not need to thank me," he muttered, seemingly embarrassed. "Anyone would have done the same."

Alessandra swallowed a smile.

"The snow has finally given way," she offered and Christian wiped his hands over his face as if to clear it of sleep.

"That is good news. You must be eager to return to your home," he said but Alessandra thought she saw a glimmer of regret in his eye.

"I am not sure where I'm going," she said truthfully. "But I would like to get back to my car and retrieve my belongings at minimum."

Christian looked up quickly.

"Why will you not return home?" he asked. "Are you in danger?"

Alessandra shook her head and offered him a quick smile. He had done enough for her. She did not need to drag him into her troubles.

"Should we go in the morning?" she asked. "Or would you prefer we go now?"

Christian rose from his winged chair.

"You remind me of someone I lost," he told her and she was stunned by the revelation.

"I do?" she asked. She could not imagine anyone confusing her with an Amish woman.

You are an actress, she reminded herself. *Technically you could be anyone at all.*

"Who?"

"My sister, Hannah. She was willful and childish like you."

Alessandra's mouth dropped open.

"Willful and childish?" she choked. "I am not – "

"And she would argue anyone for any reason whatsoever," Christian sighed. "She was a fighting spirit...until she could not fight any longer."

An unexpected sadness filled her.

"What happened to her?" she asked gently.

"She was very sick for a very long while and she no longer wanted to burden us with her pain. She took her own life."

The shock was almost a physical blow to her.

"Why are you telling me this?" she whispered. Christian stared deeply into her eyes.

"I do not know."

He turned his head and Alessandra realized he did not want her to see the tears in his eyes.

"I will wake you in the morning. Good night."

He disappeared, leaving her to stare after him, a combination of emotions flowing through her, each one more painful than the last.

At dawn, Christian knocked on the door to the small bedroom where Alex had not slept all night. She had visions of Christian's sister taking her own life, tired of fighting off whatever had plagued her.

Will I suffer the same fate? If I get tired of running? If Christian's sister was a fighter like me, could I end up like her?

"Are you ready to go?" he called to her from the hall.

"Yes," she replied, opening the door. He seemed surprised to see her fully dressed.

As they stepped into the surprisingly sunny morning, Alessandra stole a look at her savior, wondering if he would ever get over the apparent heartbreak he felt from the loss of a sister.

Their trip back to her abandoned car was quiet but for Ferd's sighs as he clomped through the fresh and sparkling snow. The day felt ripe with promise but a sense of sadness hung over the duo.

Alessandra's car was covered in snow so high, it almost reached the lowest branch of the trees on the side of Route 322.

She pulled open the driver's side door, remembering where she had left the snow brush and almost chuckled.

Had that only been three days ago? It seems like years.

She reminded herself that it was no laughing matter, that a psychopath still deigned to kill her and no amount of losing herself in the Amish life would change that.

"I'm going to see if my car will start," she told Christian who stayed on the bench of the wagon. He nodded solemnly and watched her pensively.

Her keys were still in the ignition and Alessandra chuckled to herself.

Only in Amish country can you leave keys in the ignition of an unlocked convertible for three days and it stays right where you left it.

The engine turned over after two tries, cold from sitting but otherwise unscathed.

"I think I'm okay," she called up to Christian from the driver's seat. "I'll just let it run for a few minutes to melt the snow and carry on my way."

"I will wait," he answered and she was inexplicably touched by the response.

I wonder if we would have hit it off had we met in a different life, she thought, peering up at him covertly. He seemed to be watching her in the same manner and she wondered what he was thinking.

"I'm going to call my agent," she told him. "It looks like he has been trying to reach me."

She dialled her voicemail first, noticing the plethora of missed calls. Her eyes widened in bewilderment as she listened to the influx of frenzied messages.

"Alex, it's me. Some man has turned himself into the police, claiming he tried to murder you outside the theater last night. No one has heard from you. Please call me...Miss Blaine, this is Detective Carson from the Harrisburg Police Department. We have been trying unsuccessfully to get in touch with you for days on an urgent matter. Please return our calls...Alex, it's me again, Dennis. We are freaking out..." and so the messages continued.

She hung up the phone and grinned widely at Christian.

"You seem happy," he said, eyeing her with interest. She nodded.

"I got good news," she replied. "I can go home after all."

Christian did not reply immediately.

"You have an agent?" he finally asked after a moment of awkward silence. "Are you a writer?"

"No...I'm an actress," she told him. "Didn't I mention?"

Christian shook his head.

"You have not even made mention of your name," he replied somewhat dryly. Alex's mouth dropped open.

"Wha – what?" she asked incredulously. "It's Alessandra. Alessandra Blaine."

Christian's head whipped around suddenly and he peered at her disbelievingly.

"You were in a production of *The Taming of the Shrew* in Harrisburg recently?" he demanded, his eyes wide. Alessandra's jaw dropped further.

"Yes! I just did my last show there!"

"You were magnificent as Kate!"

She burst into laughter, her voice echoing through the fields and Christian joined her, the two gazing at one another with amusement.

"Well I am sorry I didn't know you were a fan or else I would have signed an autograph for you," Alex joked but in her heart, she suddenly did not want to leave.

And what? I will stay and convert to Amish? Start up an acting troupe here in Lancaster County?

As if he was reading her thoughts, Christian spoke softly.

"I do not wish to sound bold but I daresay the roads are still quite dangerous to drive upon, especially in such a small vehicle. Perhaps you should wait one more day for the plows to go through."

Immediately Alex bobbed her head in agreement, pulling the keys from her ignition and leaping from the car to join her new friend on the wagon.

"I will trade you an autograph for that reflexology," she teased.

"It's a deal," he replied, steering Ferd back toward his farm.

Stealing another glance at Christian in her peripheral vision, Alessandra smiled.

Maybe I will be back to the Keystone State after all. Maybe I will just stay.

REBECCA'S RUMSPRINGA

ALANA MILLER

91

Rebecca stared out of the window of her bedroom, the one she shared with her younger brothers and sisters. The fields rolled before her, barren now that the harvest was over. She had begged her parents to delay the Rumspringa, until after the harvest at least, even though her birthday had just passed this summer. She had tried to convince them to let her stay, but they insisted she go.

"Rebecca, would you come here please?" her mother called from the kitchen.

"Yes, Momma." She called back and deposited her knitting into the basket at the corner of her room. Rebecca fixed her skirts, brushing off yarn hairs that were attracted to the plain navy color. She walked down the hall and into the kitchen. Her mother pulled a fresh pie out of the oven and set it on a potholder on the table.

"Rebecca, can you go down into the cellar and fetch me another can of apples? Then go and fetch your siblings from the barn for supper."

"Yes, Momma." Rebecca said, and pulled on her boots. She stalked across the ground to the barn as the sun began to dip behind the hills and trees. She could hear her younger siblings screeching and laughing in the hayloft. She pulled open the door and smelled the sweet hay and manure.

"Come on, kids. Momma says its supper time." She called to the hayloft. She heard their muffled giggles and the boards sigh as they shifted their weight behind the hay bales.

"Alright, I guess I'll just have to eat all the potatoes and carrots from the roast Momma made. I know how much Anna and Naomi and Fannie love those little sweet carrots. Too bad they're not out here." Rebecca called and turn to leave. She heard her young siblings scramble down the ladder.

They raced past her into the house. She walked behind and lingered for a few more seconds, hoping to catch a glimpse of the neighbor boy, Joshua Hostetler. He was a cute boy, nearing manhood, and possibly looking a wife soon. She would catch him glancing at her when they were both working their respective fields with their families, or when they passed each other after services. Of course, she would glance back, but sparingly.

They sat around the dinner table, her father said the blessing, they ate. Rebecca's mind wandered as she picked absentmindedly at her plate. She wondered what she would see, who she would meet. She had heard about the outside world, how crass and improper it could be. She felt her stomach drop and twist with nerves.

Rebecca changed into her nightgown and sighed. She would miss her bed, the secret cat only the kids knew about who lived in the attic, the smell of hay.

"So, Rebecca, thought about anyone dreamy lately?" Anna laid sprawled across Rebecca's bed and flipped through the pages of her diary.

"Anna, you little snot!" Rebecca lunged and snatched the diary out of danger.

"What? It's fun to read." Anna slid into her own bed.

"That's rude, Anna! You're supposed to respect others and their feelings," Rebecca said, throwing her pillow at Anna.

"Well, if you marry Joshua Hostetler, then I can't marry his younger brother. When I come of age, of course," Anna said, brushing her hair back.

"You are too young to think about such things now. As the youngest, you'll have the worst choice anyways," Rebecca teased and brushed Anna's hair. Naomi, Fannie, and Maggie sit on the bed.

"Tells us about what you and Joshua," Naomi said. Rebecca smiled softly and started to braid Anna's hair.

"Me and Joshua will live in the old King house, that beautiful one with the large attic room and the big kitchen. We'll have so many children, eight or nine. I'll make quilts for all of them and have lots of grandchildren and be the best mother and wife and grandmother.

I can't imagine anything better than just being happy and in good health with a good husband." Rebecca said. Her mind wandered to her marriage day.

She said good night to her siblings and tucked them all into bed. She crept downstairs and watched her parents sleeping for just a moment. She crept back upstairs and knelt by her bed and said her prayers.

Dear God, please watch over my family. Thank you for giving me this day and thank you for giving me tomorrow. Please let my siblings grow up strong and let my parents grow old. Please let me bless my family with lots of children and grandchildren. Please bless all my sisters with good husbands and my brothers with good wives. Thank you for this good harvest and please let next year be just as good. In your name I pray, Amen.

She got into bed and began to write in her diary. The candle light fluttered and flickered as she wrote. She wrote about her day, about tending her mother's herb garden, about the socks she was darning. She wrote about Joshua, as well, just a little bit. Then she blew out the candle and snuggled under the thick handmade quilt.

Rebecca rose before the sun, just like every other day. She dressed quickly, pulling on warm thick socks against the cool fall. She crept down the stairs slowly. Her mother sat in the rocking chair by the front door. She grabbed her mother's shoulder.

"Are you ready to go?" They both looked out the window as the sun began to color the sky.

"Yes, Momma. I'm not sure if I really want to go," Rebecca said softly. Upstairs, she could hear tiny feet stirring as her brothers and sisters woke up.

"It'll be good for you. You need to see something other than the same old farm and same old people. You don't feel restless now, but you will if you don't take this opportunity. Go be young and free so you can come home and start a family and be a good wife," her mother said, squeezing Rebecca's hand.

"So you went on your own Rumspringa, then Momma?" Rebecca knelt by her mother's chair.

"Aye. It was actually a bit boring. I went up the road to the town and stayed with a very nice English family. It was summer, and I tended their children and their house while the parents were working. They were good Christian folks. It was refreshing to get out, and see how the world works outside. But I'm sure things have changed since then," her mother said, reminiscing.

"Do you want me to get you a gift while I'm out," Rebecca joked.

"Maybe just a new recipe or some new fabric for a quilt. I'm thinking something with purple or green in it."

"Alright, Momma. I'm going to go finish packing." She kissed her mother's hand and stood. Her siblings rushed down the stairs and into the kitchen. Rebecca walked back up the stairs and finished packing her knapsack; her diary, an extra dress, two extra pairs of socks, and an extra bootlace.

She said goodbye to family when the sun finally rose. She hugged her siblings tightly. Her father hugged her tighter and longer.

"I'll miss you, little flower" he muttered.

"I'll miss you, too, Poppa," she said back into his shoulder. She kissed her mother's cheek and hugged her tightly, too.

Then she set off. She hefted her knapsack onto her shoulder and set off down the old dirt road. As she passed the Hostetler farm, Joshua waved her down from his porch. He shouldered his own pack and jogged across the yard to the road.

"Hi, Rebecca. Mind if I walk with you?"

"Not at all. How are you, Joshua?" She shifted her bag.

"I'm doing well. Let me take that for you." He grabbed her knapsack and slung it over his other shoulder.

"Are you excited," she asked, putting her hands in her pockets.

"Yeah, a little. I want to go and see a movie and taste popcorn." Rebecca glanced at him, out of the corner of her eye. He was handsome, in his dark plain shirt. She didn't feel quite pretty enough standing next him in her plain black dress. She wanted him to notice her, but she didn't want to act like those English girls who wore too much rogue and too little clothing.

"That sounds fun," she remarked lightly. Her stomach fluttered with nervous butterflies.

"What do you plan on doing?" He looked straight at her now. *Straight and honest like a good Amish man,* she thought.

"I'm going to find some fabric for my mother, and maybe some toys for my siblings. My father didn't want anything, but I'm going to find him a new book."

"Rebecca, this is a chance at freedom, not a market trip," he laughed. She liked his laugh, deep and hearty.

"Aye, I know. But I don't really want to go on this trip to begin with, so I figured I would make it a practical trip," she sulked.

"You are a proper Amish woman, if there was ever one," he chuckled and adjusted their packs.

They met Sarah at the edge of the community. They stood for a moment under the gate. Rebecca rubbed her fingers together, trying to rub a little warmth back into them.

"Good morning, Sarah." Joshua said politely.

"Good morning, Joshua. Are we ready to go," she replied. She hefted her pack high onto her shoulder and set off down the road towards town.

"I guess we're going," Rebecca muttered. She and Sarah had been friends long ago, but when Sarah made her intention clear of leaving the community, their friendship faltered. Sarah had been shunned and Rebecca had not been allowed to even talk to her friend. Rebecca had wanted to be there, to help her friend through what must've been a hard time to come to the decision to leave the only community she knew.

They tromped down the road side by side. Cars zoomed by, some honked, some had teens leaning out windows and yelling at them. Someone even threw trash at them. Rebecca took Sarah's hand. She didn't take Joshua's. When they made it into town, the sun was high overhead. Between them, they had a little over $70.

"Do you know where we should go? Or what we're supposed to do?" Rebecca looked between Sarah and Joshua.

"We find a place called a hotel. We get a room for the night. Then tomorrow I'm going to the city. You two can do whatever," Sarah said disdainfully.

"What's in the city?" Joshua fixed a stern look at Sarah.

"A publishing house. I'm going to be a writer, a famous writer. I'll cut my hair short and wear pants." Sarah remarked. She shifted her bag and stalked off down the street. She glanced over her shoulder at Rebecca and Joshua, then ducked into a restaurant. Joshua looked at Rebecca and shrugged. They followed her down the sidewalk and into the restaurant. As they sat down at a table, Rebecca noticed the strange looks they garnered. The young waitress who took their orders gave them curious glances from across the restaurant. Her name tag said Helen. She was short and petite, with long blond wavy hair pulled back into a high ponytail.

"I'm sorry to stare, but you're Amish, right?" The waitress looked at them, with the same curiosity of a child seeing a lion at the zoo for the first time. She had a strange accent, drawing out some of the vowels.

"Yes, we're out on Rumspringa, which is like a journey Amish youth take before becoming full-fledged members of the community." Rebecca smiled sweetly at the girl.

"That's pretty cool. A lot of local kids just go to the big city for a couple months before coming back here. Some of them go to college and meet people, then come back and settle down. "

"What do they do in the big city?" Sarah said, her eyes shining brightly.

"Party usually. They just do stupid stuff and pretend that they're adults. It's boring, really." Helen shrugged.

"So, what do you local kids do?" Joshua said, giving the waitress a strange half-smile. Rebecca felt a strange thread of jealousy. *He's never given me a smile like that,* she thought. She considered pouting, but she was an adult now, she didn't need to pout.

"We go to the library and the movies and the mall in the next town over. Sometimes I hit up a barn party on the other side town. Just every now and then. It's kind of fun." Helen shrugged again.

After they ate, Sarah dragged Rebecca towards the back of the restaurant, towards Helen.

"Helen, right? I'm Sarah and this Rebecca. I was wondering, I don't want to impose, but do you know where there's a store nearby? I don't think we brought enough clothes and we just need to pick up something to blend in a little better."

"Oh, yeah. There's a place just a few doors down. If you want to wait just a little longer, I'll be off work and I can get my friends Alex and Tiffany to help us out. Alex loves shopping," She said, trailing off a little at the end.

"Oh, thank you, but on second thought, I think we can manage on our own," Rebecca stuttered nervously.

"Are you sure? I seriously don't mind," Helen said.

"Yes, we'll be fine. We don't need to impose on your charity," Rebecca said, more forceful now.

"Alright. I'm not very familiar with how things work out in the boonies up here, but I'm from the South. Besides racism and comfort food, we have hospitality. That means we take care of our guests." She took her apron and flung it on the counter.

"Delilah, I'm taking my lunch now!" Helen grabbed Sarah and Rebecca's wrists and dragged them out of the restaurant. Joshua scrambled after them. Helen pulled out, what Rebecca assumed was her phone, and tapped on the rectangular glass repeatedly.

"Alex, I need you to drop everything and meet us downtown now." She paused. "No, fashion emergency. And get Tiffany down here too." She paused again. "Yes, yes. I'll see you in a moment." She pushed the rectangle back into her pants pocket.

She pulled the two girls after her, down the smooth sidewalk. Joshua jogged to keep up with them. Helen pushed the two girls into a small corner shop that was mostly windows. The shop was packed with clothing racks that erupted fabric of all shapes, sizes, and colors. Even from all the stories and scant images, Rebecca could still barely believe all the colors and fabrics stretching before her.

Helen set about pulling article after article from the racks. A bored looking youth manned the counter. Rebecca couldn't tell much about the youth; they had short chopped up colored hair, and scary spikes through their eyebrows and ears. Rebecca was intimidated by them. But they made her feel overexposed; that typical English teen made her feel so out place. Joshua watched as Helen piled clothes on both of the girls. She then pushed them into tiny cubicles and closed the doors.

"Start trying those things on. I had to guess at a lot of your sizes, since those dresses don't do you girls any justice," Helen yelled and threw the piles over the top of the door.

Rebecca looked through everything. *How does anybody get anything done when they have to spend so much time picking out clothes and then putting them on,* she thought to herself as she stripped out of her dress. She picked up the first thing that caught her eye and glared at it. It was purple and strangely strappy. She couldn't decide if it was a sweater or a scarf.

"Helen? I think I need some help," Sarah called from her closet. Rebecca heard the chuckle from Helen.

"Luckily the cavalry has arrived, ladies," Helen chuckled and opened the door a crack.

"Rebecca, honey, this is Alex. She's going to help you get into those things. I didn't even think about the whole culture shock thing." Helen shoved a tall, slim girl into the changing room. The girl was dark skinned and had curly hair. Rebecca wanted to know how she got her hair to curl like that. Alex had a small gold stud piercing in the side of her nose.

"Hi, I'm Alex." She held out her hand to Rebecca. Rebecca took it and shook her hand like she had seen men do.

"Here, let me help you into that. Aren't you going to take that off?" Alex eyed the slip Rebecca wore.

"No? This is like our, uh, underwear." Rebecca blushed fiercely.

"Oh, okay. Then try this on instead." Alex handed her a bright blue sweater that Rebecca did like over the purple one. They spent hours cramming themselves into strange clothes. Rebecca felt like the English girls spoke a whole different language as they passed clothes back and forth to Sarah and Rebecca.

Size 4 instead of 6...

Grunge, not punk...

No, darker...

No, lighter...

Pastels...

More sparkles, Less sparkles...

At the end of the ordeal, Rebecca and Sarah muttered to each other and counted their money. The number crept higher and higher. Rebecca felt like her heart was going to explode and her stomach twisted in knots. They stepped up to the counter, ready to face the music. Helen pushed her way between them.

"Girls, put your damn money away right now." She slapped a plastic card on the counter top and glared over her shoulder at the two girls who clutched their money nervously.

"But, Helen –," Rebecca started.

"No. Away with it." The rectangle was swiped in the machine and the cashier bagged their clothes up. Joshua was leaning wearily against the wall. Rebecca picked up her bag of clothes. The plastic felt greasy and slick on her palm. Shame crept up her neck. As they exited the store, Rebecca wanted to turn and run.

"Thank you, Helen, for your generosity. We'll be on our way now." Rebecca looked down to avoid eye contact with Helen. Helen grabbed her shoulder.

"Let's go. My place is just a couple blocks away."

"Helen, we can't impose on you anymore," Joshua laid his hand over Helen's.

"It's not imposing. When you make new friends, you're supposed to take care of them. Tonight that means going to my house, sleeping in my beds, and eating my food." She winked at Joshua and squeezed Rebecca's arm gently. Alex pulled up to the curb in her car, a silver 4 door car.

They piled in; Helen sat in the front passenger seat and the other 4 into the back. Tiffany and Sarah sat squished against one door. Rebecca sat between the other door and Joshua. Joshua's leg pressed against hers snuggly. When they took corners too sharply, because Alex was not a very good driver, he would press harder against her. Rebecca could feel the heat in her face. She kept her eyes carefully fixed on studying the pattern of the back of the seat. Then he leaned over, on purpose.

"How do you feel about your first car ride," he whispered.

"It's a little hot and cramped. Do you think all car rides are this way?" He chuckled lowly in her ear. She could feel his breath on her neck. Her faced flared brilliant red as her thoughts began to race. *I wonder what it would feel like to kiss him at this moment...* She mentally chastised herself and sent a prayer to God, asking for forgiveness of her lust.

They stopped outside a two-story house. It was pastel yellow. There were large windows all across the front. Alex pulled into the driveway and parked. Rebecca fumbled with the door latch before finally squeezing it enough to open the door. She slid out of the car and onto the front lawn gracelessly. She straightened her skirts and brushed some wrinkles out. Her hands felt clammy and shook a little. She grabbed her old knapsack and her new plastic bag filled with new clothes.

"Your house is very large," Joshua observed. His eyes darted all around the house.

"Really? This is like a smaller house on this block. It's got like 3 bedrooms and only 1 bathroom. The back yard is a nice size though, good for a small or medium dog," Tiffany shrugged and walked up the stairs of the front porch.

"You lock the doors around here?" Rebecca stared at the chain of keys Tiffany picked through.

"Yeah? You don't?" Tiffany looked at Rebecca like she had just sprouted feathers. Rebecca had never needed to lock doors at home; they were a community and no one needed to steal anything.

They all pushed through the door. Sarah, Joshua, and Rebecca stood in the doorway, watching the three young women. Tiffany turned lights on all over the place. Rebecca played with one of the switches and watched the light flick on and off above her. Alex and Helen stand in the kitchen, tapping away on their phones.

"Okay, I'll get the girls set up in the spare bed. But where will we put sweet little Joshy?" Alex said and winked at Joshua. His face turned scarlet. Rebecca couldn't help but glare at her. Tiffany bumped her arm.

"Don't worry, she's teasing. She's very involved with her long-time boyfriend Thomas. They'll probably get married someday, but she's having too much fun being young," Tiffany whispered. She offered Rebecca a sweet smile. Rebecca and Sarah trudged up the stairs after Alex. She opened a door at the end of the hall, second door on the left, Rebecca noted.

"Sorry, there's only one bed. I hope that's not an issue." Alex glanced between the two girls.

"No, sisters share bed until one of the gets married." Sarah said and slid past Alex. Alex grabbed Rebecca's arm though.

"I saw your face downstairs. If I was out of line, I'm sorry. But if you would like, I can show you a thing or two about wooing a prospective male." Alex smiled sweetly down at Rebecca. Rebecca offered her an awkward half-smile and edged into the bedroom. They spread their new cloths out on the bed.

"These cloths are so weird. They don't feel... right," Rebecca said and ran her fingers across the clothes. Sarah shrugged and stripped out of her dress. She pulled on her new clothes quickly. Sarah looked in the mirror above the dresser and pulled off her prayer cap.

"I like them." Sarah left the room. Rebecca gaped at her. Then she stripped off her own clothes and pulled on the black slacks and baby blue sweater. She looked in the mirror too. She saw a young girl staring back, one who was afraid of her future. The stark white prayer cap covered her brown hair. She also removed the cap and her hair fell into a long braid down her back.

Rebecca walked down the stairs slowly. Her gut knotted when she thought of what Joshua would think of her. Only married couples saw a woman's hair. She walked into the kitchen, in only her sock covered feet. Sarah and Tiffany sat at the table, talking about her hair. Helen opened a rectangular box and Rebecca felt her stomach grumble.

"Here, this is the most American food that has ever existed. Pizza!" She held a slice covered in pepperoni out to her. Rebecca took a bite out of the cheesy triangle. The hot cheese burned her tongue but tasted amazing. She smiled and nodded at Helen's expectant face. But pizza was forgotten in a snap; Joshua walked in a plain white t-shirt and dark blue jeans. Rebecca's face flared again and she looked down, away from him.

"Rebecca..." He didn't finish that thought. The unspoken intimacy between them, felt by only them, created tension that pervaded the room. Alex cleared her throat loudly.

"So, there's a party going on tonight, if you guys want to hit it up? We can finish some pizza and get out there," Helen said, leaning heavily on the table.

"Yeah, let's go!" Sarah lit up.

"Okay, that's settled. Let's go get ready, ladies. Joshua, you look great already." Alex winked at him again and herded the girls up the stairs. Joshua's eyes never left Rebecca.

Upstairs, in Alex's bedroom, Sarah and Rebecca were subject to poking and prodding, being stuffed into strange tight dresses. Rebecca pulled on the strange tights under her short dress. They made her miss her thick, comfy socks. The English girls smeared her face with make-up; reddened her lips and lined her eyes in thick black lines. They pulled her hair and curled it and brushed it. Rebecca couldn't recognize herself after they were done with her.

She walked down the stairs holding onto Helen's arm. Joshua looked up at her from the bottom of the stairs. He looked a little disappointed, but he didn't take his eyes off her. Rebecca felt a small sliver of pride knowing that Joshua only had eyes for her. They piled into Alex's car and drove off to the party. Rebecca felt a little more comfortable this time, sitting next to Joshua. *I'm almost in his lap, What am I supposed to do if something like that happens?*

They walked up to the barn. Joshua was still taller than her in her ridiculous shoes that squeezed her toes and made her ankles feel weak. *Or maybe Joshua is why my ankles feel weak,* she thought to herself with a secret smile. Loud music pounded and Rebecca could feel it in her heart, like a second heartbeat. Inside, there were barely any lights. Rebecca could see teens dancing with each other; it looked like animals mating. She wanted to turn and leave. Helen pushed a plastic cup into her hand and demanded she drink it.

The alcohol burned her throat. She gagged and coughed. Joshua was whisked away into the party by several guys that Alex and Helen knew. Rebecca leaned against a wall and watched teens kiss and grind and drink. *This isn't the place for me...* Someone grabbed her arm and startled her.

"It's just me," Joshua screamed over the music. Rebecca smiled at him. He took her hand and led her outside.

"Sorry, I just needed some air. Are you having fun?" He looked her up and down. He smelled of alcohol.

"No, but this will be a story to tell my kids and grandchildren," she chuckled.

"Let's take a walk." He took her hand again and led her down road. They walked for a few minutes. Then Joshua slipped his hand over her rear. She pushed him away forcefully.

"Joshua!" Rebecca stared at Joshua, her heart pounded against her ribs. Her stomach churned from the alcohol.

"I'm sorry. This is just a, a misunderstanding!" He glanced around. Panic was setting in and shone in his eyes.

"What do you mean, a misunderstanding? You've brought me out here in the middle of the night and for what? To catch our death of cold? And you gave me that nasty poison, for what? To drag me down into the filth and sin with Sarah? And then you try to start something that I gave no intention of wanting!" Rebecca felt the panic rise in her throat.

"I'm sorry, Rebecca. I didn't mean to. It was a stupid dare from those English boys I was hanging out with. I just wanted a chance to be alone with you." Joshua looked down. Even in the dark, Rebecca saw the blush creep across his face.

"Why? If you had wanted to talk to me, you could've said so!" Rebecca yelled, exasperated.

"I just didn't know how to talk to you. And those English boys were trying to convince me to 'make my move' on you." Joshua shoved his hands in his pockets.

"Oh Joshua," Rebecca sighed. The cold was starting to chill her.

Rebecca held the coat tightly against her body. She felt so small at that moment. *God, please watch over me and Joshua for what we are about to do,* she prayed silently. She shivered slightly.

"Joshua, come on. Let's go. We can walk to town in just a few hours," Rebecca said, holding out her hand. Joshua took it, his large calloused hand enveloped her smaller one. Her heart pounded even harder now.

"You shouldn't be walking in those ridiculous shoes," he remarked. She was wearing ridiculous shoes. "But you do look nice tonight," he added. She blushed and looked away from him.

"Do you think we'll be okay, being out here on our own?" She left out the rest of her thought. *Do you think we'll okay without a chaperone?*

"I hope so, Rebecca. This has got to be the worst Rumspringa in the history of ever." Joshua squeezed her hand gently. She hoped her heart wouldn't jump out of her chest.

"The first Rumspringa was probably terrible," she said, with a chuckle," Because back then, the English lived just like us, so it was probably just boring to leave." She laughed.

"That is a very good point," he said back.

"Have you thought what you'll do when we get back?"

"Yeah. I'm going to apprentice under Miles Yoder and learn how to care for cattle and such. I think it would be easier to have livestock than to tend a field." She watched him out of the corner of her eye. She liked seeing his eyes sparkle and she could see the thoughts racing through his head. She had much of the same thoughts constantly racing through her head.

"Have you thought about who you would like to marry, someday," Rebecca said, trying to be casual, nonchalant.

"Yeah, just a passing thought or two. You?" He squeezed her hand again. She squeezed his back. Her feet started to hurt now and her fingers had started to burn from the cold.

"Yeah, every now and then." She said, looking at him. He stopped and looked at her. Their English clothes were dirty from tromping through the dark woods. She felt tired in ways she couldn't have imagined.

"Rebecca," he whispered. It wasn't a question or a statement. He said it like he just wanted to hear her name from his own two lips.

"Yes, Joshua?" She felt like there were swarms off bees in her belly, buzzing and fluttering.

"Who do you think about when you think about your future?" He stepped ever so slightly closer.

"You really want to know?" She smiled up at him. She loved his jaw, his grey-green eyes she could barely see in the dark, the way his hair curled and the shadow of facial hair that had begun to grow.

"Yes."

"Kiss me," she whispered. Her heart pounded so hard against her ribs. His hands crept under her coat, but stayed on her waist. He pulled her close. She slipped up onto tiptoes, trying to get closer faster. But her ridiculous shoes had other plans. She stumbled into him.

"Sorry, I don't know what I thinking." She giggled and rested her head on his shoulder.

"I do," he said. His rough fingers turned her chin up slightly. Her breath caught in her throat as he leaned forward ever so slightly. It felt like time stopped in that moment. Her heart beat once, twice and then his lips finally brushed against hers. It was so soft, so gentle, so short. *Again*, she thought.

"Again? You sure?" He joked.

"I didn't mean to say that out loud," she laughed and clutched his jacket," do you think we'll get in trouble? I don't think that was allowed."

"If nobody knows, then I think we'll be okay."

Joshua put his arms around her and hugged her tight. She hugged him back.

"When we get back, we'll have to do things proper. All the courtship traditions and such," Joshua said, "Do you think your father will allow me to marry you?"

"Probably. He thinks your father is a good man, and will give me over willingly. I do like how the English move through courtship. That Alex girl has been with her boyfriend for many years, but they didn't have to hide it or ask any permission of anyone. And they divorce all the time!" Rebecca shivered in her coat.

"I know! Imagine if any of the women did that at home! The shunning, the outrage," Joshua said dramatically.

"Imagine if we went through courtship like the English! Kissing on the first meeting, married by the third, having children by the time we were together three months, then splitting up by our first anniversary," Rebecca draped herself against Joshua. Her feet hurt in those shoes, but she knew if she took them off she would only be colder.

"We wouldn't split up. You're stuck with me now, Miss Fisher." Joshua stopped and looked at her again. "If you'll have me, that is." His eyes were full of hope.

"Are you asking me to marry you, Joshua Hostetler?" Rebecca was cold and hot all at once. Tonight had been such a strange night.

"Aye," he whispered. Her cold fingers grasped his.

"Then aye, I'll have you," She whispered back.

"Then let's get back to town and back home."

"First, another kiss?" she asked quietly.

"Of course, my dear," he replied softly. His lips brushed against hers so softly and gently. She didn't know if it had been the alcohol in her body or love, but she leaned further into it. The kiss edged from adorable and chaste to passionate and fiery. Rebecca understood why English girls kissed boys all the time; it felt hot and intense. She felt like time stopped around them. She no longer felt her cold fingers and cold toes. It was addictive to be so close to him, to be just the two of them in that moment. He pushed her away gently.

"I'm sorry. Forgive me, I acted improperly," She whispered. Shame flared across her face. She couldn't bring her eyes to meet his. He chuckled slightly.

"So did I. Let's get back to town, you're freezing." He kissed her forehead. He took her hand and led her back to town and to the warm beds waiting for them.

"Hey, Joshua, want to hear something really funny?" Rebecca pushed her face against his arm.

"Sure," he chuckled.

"I'm not wearing any underwear!" Rebecca giggled.

"Come on, you need to sober up." He wrapped an arm around her shoulder and they walked home.

The next day, they all stood outside the restaurant. Joshua held Rebecca's hand tightly. They had changed back into their Amish clothing, their normal clothing. Sarah looked so strange from when she had arrived just a few days earlier; she had shorn her long brown hair so short, into what Alex called a 'pixie' cut, and was wearing typical English clothing. Rebecca was sad to see her friend leave, but was happy she had found where she belonged. *Dear God, please watch Sarah as she walks a different path,* she prayed silently.

"Okay, you crazy kids. Be safe, don't fall off your horses and such. I'll be stopping by in the future to see your wedding, and oh- meeting your children!" Helen sobbed a little. Rebecca hugged her close.

"Aye, we'll be waiting for you. We'll send out invitations with all the dates and such. Amish have very intensive courtship traditions." Rebecca wiped a stray tear from her own face.

"I hope we're invited, too," Alex asked and hugged Rebecca tightly and then hugged Joshua tightly.

"Of course. Everyone will be invited. It'll be the biggest wedding, with Amish and English sitting down and celebrating our marriage," Joshua exclaimed and hugged Rebecca tightly. She couldn't help but giggle.

"Now get out of here! Go get to courting!" Helen sniffled and pushed them gently. They walked down the road, hand in hand. Their future was bright, and almost in their grasp. Just a few more steps down the road. Rebecca saw their lives playing out in front of them, the happiest in Joshua's face on their wedding day, the purity of the wedding night, the joy of their first year together and of their first child. On and on, their lives would be happy and peaceful. Rebecca was content to know that she was on her path and she had the man of her dreams next to her for every step of the journey.

A LEAP OF FAITH

STEPHANIE SWIFT

Hope Miller laced her fingers together on top of her lap and did her best to empty her mind so she could focus on Bishop Abram's sermon.

It wasn't an easy task.

Sitting to her right was her mother and father, both of whom sat with rigid backs and facial expressions as hard and stern as the wooden pew they were seated on. To her left were her aunt Martha and uncle Seth, who both appeared comfortable and at ease, holding hands and smiling as they listened to the message. The two couples couldn't be more opposite if they tried, and she felt like neutral ground between them, which was disconcerting to say the least.

Hope cautiously looked over her right shoulder and smiled at Noah Wyse, her closest friend and ally. He sat a couple of pews behind them on the other side of the sanctuary with his six-year-old daughter, Ivy, who gave her a shy wave when she caught Hope looking their way. She wanted to wave back at her, but she knew if her mother or father caught her goofing off during the service she would never hear the end of it.

Noah gave her a sympathetic smile, and she turned her attention back to Bishop Abram before she made the mistake of smiling back at him and causing an uproar if one of the elders of the church caught her doing it. Even though she and Noah were just friends, it was highly frowned upon in their small Amish community for the unmarried men and women to cavort with each other unless they were promised to marry. It was ridiculous, really, but the last thing she wanted to do was cause a scene.

Hope sighed. If only things were simpler and less complicated. At twenty years old, she was one of the oldest from her generation who hadn't married, but that didn't bother her in the least. After growing up in a home with parents who shared a loveless marriage, a relationship was the furthest thing from her mind. Because of their strict faith, divorce was next to impossible, but there were many times during her youth when she wished her parents would go their separate ways. She couldn't imagine what brought the two of them together, unless it was an arranged courtship, because there was no way to picture them ever being in love.

Her aunt and uncle, on the other hand, were the epitome of love and devotion. You could see it in the way they looked at each other that their love was real. When Hope made the decision to leave home three years prior and move in with her aunt and uncle to help with her quilting business, the relief she felt was overwhelming. Gone were the days stepping on egg shells around her parents and living in a home that was so cold she could feel it in her bones. With Hope being their only child, she could only imagine how depressing the atmosphere must be now that they were alone together, and the thought made her heart ache.

No, she would never get married. Not if it meant she would lose a piece of herself and spend the rest of her days wishing for her freedom. No man was worth that.

Her mother nudged her side, startling her and making her jump. She hadn't realized she'd drifted off into her own little world, but the service was nearly over and every head in the room was bowed as Bishop Abram said his closing prayer. Hope shut her eyes as her cheeks burned hot from embarrassment. As soon as the Bishop said "amen", and everyone started for the door, her mother was on her case.

"Honestly, Hope...do you ever stop daydreaming?" she muttered.

Hope took a deep breath to keep from saying something she regretted. "I'm sorry, mother."

As they stood in line for the door, she glanced around the room in search of Noah and Ivy, but didn't find them. Hope peered through one of the church windows to see if they had already left the church, and she spotted them near a grove of trees with Victoria Kaufmann, a young widow from their area. While Noah and Victoria talked, Ivy played close by on a tire swing hanging from an old oak tree.

The two of them were deep in conversation about something, and when Victoria reached out and touched Noah's arm, Hope's temper bristled in response, which caught her off guard. *What was that about?* she wondered. She and Noah had never been romantically involved, and it wasn't the first time a single woman had flirted with Noah since his wife, Maria, passed away not long after Ivy was born.

"Are you alright?"

Hope looked behind her at her aunt Sadie, who was eyeing her skeptically. "*Yah*. Why do you ask?"

Sadie shrugged and smiled. "You just seemed puzzled for some reason."

Puzzled was putting it lightly, but Hope shook her head to clear her thoughts and to keep from dwelling on it. She and Noah were just friends, and it was probably just her over-protectiveness getting the best of her anyway. She knew very well how desperate some of her single friends were when it came to marriage, and she didn't want to see Noah hurt. That was all. He and Ivy had been through enough.

When they finally made their way outside, Hope and her aunt and uncle followed her parents to their horse and carriage to see them off, and Hope forced herself not to look in Noah and Victoria's direction.

"Sister, we would love for you and William to join us for lunch."

Hope rolled her eyes heavenward. It was the same thing every Sunday, and it always ended the same way - with her parents refusing. She would never understand how her aunt Sadie could be so patient with them when they treated her so callously.

Her mother and father stopped walking and turned to look at them. Her lips were pursed and her roughly chiseled face was set in her usual sour expression. Her father's face held no expression whatsoever.

"*Denki*, Sadie, but I'm afraid we'll have to decline. Hope, may I speak to you in private?"

Hope inhaled sharply and glimpsed at her aunt Sadie, who appeared just as perplexed. It was odd for her mother to want to talk to her about anything, much less alone. When she grabbed Hope's elbow and roughly led her a few feet away, she held her breath, expecting the worst.

"When are you coming home?" her mother asked.

Hope furrowed a brow as she pulled away from her mother's grasp. "What do you mean? I don't plan on moving back home. We've already discussed this."

Her mother huffed and puffed as she crossed her arms haughtily over her chest. "You need to stop being a burden to your aunt and uncle."

Hope took a step back. Her mother was never one to mince words, but her accusation stung. She looked over at her aunt and uncle, who were unsuccessfully trying to pull her father into conversation.

"I'm not a burden to them. How can you say that?"

Her mother wouldn't be swayed. "You're an adult, and you can't live with them forever. It's time for you to grow up and find a husband while there's still time."

Hope blinked twice. "While there's still time? You mean, while I'm still young enough to snag one?"

She didn't want to be disrespectful, but this time her mother was close to crossing the line. There was a significant difference between being concerned and acting downright rude. She hated to consider that she might be right. Did her aunt Martha and uncle Seth really consider her a burden? They'd never said anything about her overstaying her welcome, but perhaps they were just being nice.

Hope felt her eyes sting with hot tears, but she blinked them back, refusing to let her mother see that she'd gotten under her skin. Fortunately, she turned and walked back to the group before Hope had the chance to say anything further, which was probably for the best. The last place she wanted to fight with her was in the church yard with the whole congregation listening in.

She cast a wayward glance in Noah's direction, but he was still busy talking to Victoria Kaufmann and oblivious to everything else. Ivy noticed her right away and gave her a big wave as she swung back and forth on the tire swing with a silly grin highlighting her beautiful little face. Hope waved back before resigning herself to return to her family.

* * * *

Noah leaned slightly to his left so he could peek over Victoria's shoulder, and he felt his blood boil when he saw Hope talking to her mother. Actually, her mother was doing most of the talking, and he could tell from the sullen look on her face that the woman wasn't happy...as usual.

"Noah? Is something wrong?"

Her turned his attention back to Victoria, feeling guilty that he'd let his thoughts roam elsewhere. Victoria was a sweet woman, and even though he had no interest in anything other than friendship, it was obvious she felt differently. It may have been a long time since he was with another woman, but he knew flirting when he saw it.

"I'm so sorry. What were you saying?" he asked.

Victoria touched his arm again, something he noticed she was doing quite frequently while they talked. Any other man may have enjoyed it, but he'd already been blessed with the love of his life, and he wouldn't risk his heart being broken again. Plus, there was his daughter to think about, and he was far more concerned with her well-being than anything else.

"I asked if you were planning on attending the charity auction this Saturday. I'll be donating a picnic lunch."

So that was what she was getting at. It was all perfectly clear now. The auction was being held to raise money toward new books and other materials for their community schoolhouse, and it was tradition for the single women to make picnic lunches to be auctioned off among the single men. The winner would then share the lunch with the woman who donated it.

"*Yah*, I hope I can. It just depends on if I get my orders finished in time."

It wasn't a lie. Being the only blacksmith in the area, there was seldom a weekend that passed where he wasn't busy working overtime to finish orders. Not only did he have orders to complete for his neighbors, but several shop owners in nearby Lancaster were faithful customers too.

"Well, perhaps I'll see you there," she replied.

She gave him a shy smile before she turned and walked away, and Noah expelled a long breath. He stole a glance at Ivy as she played on the tire swing, and his heart swelled twice its size when she grinned back at him. She favored her mother so much it was hard not to look at her without feeling a deep pang in his chest.

He ached for the things she was missing out on not having her mother in her life. It wouldn't be long before she was a teenager, and even though he did his best to tend to her every need, there was a special bond a mother and daughter shared that he could never fill and he knew that. Ivy needed a woman in her life, and even though he missed the closeness and companionship a relationship provided, he just couldn't bear the thought of taking such a huge risk.

Noah caught sight of Hope and her aunt and uncle as he steered their horse and wagon out of the church yard and right on the main road, headed for home. Hope sat on the far right of the seat with her hands clasped together on her lap, staring off into the distance. Of all the women he knew, she was the only one he considered a close friend he could talk to and rely on. He'd bent her ear many times since Maria's passing, and she'd been there for Ivy more times than he could count.

If only they were on the same path. It wasn't as if he'd never considered the two of them as a couple, because he had many times, but Hope's parents made her jaded to the whole concept of love and marriage. Noah, on the other hand, knew the depths of love and what he stood to lose if he went down that road again, and it frightened him more than he cared to admit.

"Are you ready to go, daddy?"

Ivy appeared by his side, and when she placed her small hand in his, he forced the troubling thoughts from his mind and smiled at her. She needed him more than anyone else in his life now, and that was all that mattered. Everything else would have to wait.

* * * *

"I can't believe I'm doing this," Hope remarked.

She grimaced when she saw her friends standing in line at the auction, each of them appearing anxious as they waited to turn over their picnic baskets to Bishop Abram, who was serving as the auctioneer for the event. They were all clothed in what looked like brand-new dresses and bonnets, and they looked excited - giddy even.

"Oh, stop. It's all for a worthy cause. Did I ever tell you this is how your uncle Seth and I met?'

Hope looked beside her at her aunt Sadie, and she attempted a smile but failed miserably. If it hadn't been for her aunt's incessant nagging, she never would have agreed to taking part in such a silly tradition, but she'd come too far to back out now.

"Just look at those single men over there staring at you. I think they're memorizing what your basket looks like so they can bid on it."

Her aunt giggled as she said it, but when Hope saw the gentlemen she was referring to, her heart sank. There was Gabriel, one of the most conceited men in town, who thought he was God's gift to women, and there was Amos, a man three years younger than her who was at least a foot shorter than her too.

There were several other men in the group, but she didn't know most of them. She noticed Noah standing a few feet away, but she doubted he would take part in any of the festivities since he never had before. She'd managed to get out of it over the past four years, but her aunt had such a vise-like grip on her arm, she knew running wouldn't be an option this time around.

"Aunt Sadie, can I ask you something? I want you to be completely honest with me too."

Her aunt gave her a curious look before nodding.

"Am I a burden to you and uncle Seth?"

Her aunt tightened her grip and turned her around so they were face-to-face. Hope could tell by the look in her eyes that her question upset her.

"Of course not. You've never been a burden to us. Why would you even ask such a thing? Has my sister been filling your head with nonsense again?"

Hope smiled. Her aunt Sadie could always sense when something was bothering her, especially when it had to do with her mother. The two women were like night and day and had supposedly never gotten along during their childhood. As adults they merely tolerated each other, but it wasn't as if her aunt didn't try to build a relationship between the two of them. It was her mother who refused to budge.

"We love having you with us, and there's no way I could run my quilting business without you. You've been a Godsend, and don't you dare let your mother tell you any different. Now...get over there and get in line."

She gave her a little push and Hope had no choice but to do as she said. She made her way to the end of the line, literally dragging her feet with every step. If someone like Gabriel or Amos won her basket it would be the longest picnic lunch of her life. Hopefully, someone she could at least put up with for an hour or so would bid on her basket and win.

When Hope inched her way to the front of the line and handed over her basket to Bishop Abram, he looked surprised to see her. "I'm glad you're participating this year, Hope."

She prayed her feelings weren't painfully obvious on her face because she hated to disappoint him. Not trusting herself to speak, she simply smiled at him before making her way back to her aunt Sadie.

There were several other fundraising festivities taking place, and since the auction wasn't scheduled for at least another hour, the two of them walked around admiring the assorted pies, cookies, and other goods for sale. Hope tried not to dwell on the upcoming auction and have fun, especially since social gatherings were far and few between in her little community.

"Looks like Noah will have his hands full deciding who he's going to have lunch with," Sadie said.

Hope followed her gaze to the makeshift stage where the auction was going to be held. Noah stood off to the side of the stage, where he was flanked by three women – Victoria and two other women she didn't recognize. All four of them were talking and laughing, and the women's intentions were obvious by the way they batted their eyelashes at him and stood so close to him she wondered how he could breathe.

"It looks that way," she replied.

For reasons she couldn't explain, seeing the women fawn over him made her uneasy. The thought that he might be interested in one of them brought with it the realization that although they were good friends, it probably wouldn't always be that way, especially if he remarried. After all, what woman would put up with her husband having a close friendship with another woman, no matter how innocent it might be?

"Something troubling you?"

She turned to her aunt, who was eyeing her with an amused look on her face.

"No. Why do you ask?"

Her aunt put her hands on her hips and laughed. "Really, Hope? I have a tough time believing you don't feel a tad bit jealous seeing those women flirt with Noah. You had this same look on your face at church when you saw him talking to Victoria."

Hope's jaw slacked. That was crazy. Why in the world would she be jealous? They were just friends and nothing more. He'd mentioned many times how he wasn't interested in dating again, and...well, there was no way she would risk becoming as unhappy as her mother.

Before she could redeem herself, Bishop Abram was taking the stage and ushering everyone to sit down. Several of the pews from the church had been brought outside for the auction and as Hope and Sadie sat down on the middle row, she noticed Noah making his way to the back, were he stood behind the last pew. He waved at her when he caught her staring at him, and Hope waved back quickly and turned around to face the front, hoping he didn't see her cheeks burning red from embarrassment.

As soon as everyone was seated, Bishop Abram made his way to the podium and the table beside it that was littered with more baskets than she could count. She'd considered the number of single women donating to the auction, but she'd forgotten about the handful of widows, young and old, who might be participating – including Victoria Kaufmann.

Hope searched for her in the crowd and found her sitting near the front. When Victoria turned around in her seat, there was no denying her gaze was centered on Noah as a huge smile spread across her face. Even though Hope wanted to look at him to see what his reaction was, she forced herself not to, especially since her aunt Sadie was watching her every move.

Bishop Abram welcomed everyone to the auction before picking up the first basket – a large red wicker basket that he noted was loaded to the brim with homemade goodies like chicken and dumplings and blackberry cobbler. The bidding started at five dollars, and it didn't take long for the price to climb as several men placed their bids. It eventually sold for forty dollars to an older gentleman named Aaron, who'd been a widower for many years.

When Hope saw Clara, a middle-aged widow, pick up the basket and make her way over to Aaron and sit down, she wondered if she was the only one who detected the sly grin that passed between the two of them. She had to admit it was adorable, and part of her was kind of envious of them too.

The auction continued for at least an hour before Bishop Abram finally picked up Hope's basket. There were only three remaining, and Victoria was also waiting for hers to be called. She noticed Noah hadn't placed a bid on anything, which meant he was probably waiting on

Victoria, and that bothered her more than it probably should have. Amos had, thankfully, already bid on and won a basket, so he was out of the bidding, but Gabriel hadn't, and that made her very nervous, especially when he turned and looked her way. The wink he gave her made her nauseous, and she considered running for the hills, but her aunt Sadie wouldn't hear of it.

"The winner of this basket will be treated to a fine lunch, complete with fried chicken, fresh corn on the cob, biscuits, pecan pie, and lemonade. Let's start the bidding at five dollars," Bishop Abram said.

Just as she feared, Gabriel waved his hand in the air.

"Five dollars!" Bishop Abram yelled. "Can I get ten dollars?"

A man she didn't know took the bid, but Gabriel trumped him by bidding twenty dollars. Hope started feeling sick to her stomach. *This couldn't be happening.* The two men kept going back and forth for what seemed like forever, and she could tell that Gabriel was getting annoyed.

"Who is that man?" Hope whispered, pointing to the other bidder. "I don't recognize him."

"He just moved here about a month ago," Sadie replied. "He bought the Troyer's old dairy farm."

Hope sighed. It was bad enough that she might be forced into having lunch with someone as obnoxious as Gabriel, but trying to find something to talk about with a stranger wasn't a fun option either.

"Sixty dollars!" Bishop Abram called.

Gabriel once again raised his hand, and when the Bishop asked for sixty-five, the other gentleman didn't make a move and neither did anyone else. It was the highest bid of the auction so far, which probably should have made her happy, but not under the current circumstances. Gabriel looked her way and the smug grin on his face made her stomach twist into knots.

"Sixty dollars going once, going twice…"

"One hundred dollars!"

Hope inhaled sharply, as did most of the crowd, when someone's voice boomed from the back row. She felt her heart catch in her throat. That wasn't just any voice. She would know it anywhere. Turning slowly in her seat, Hope saw Noah with his hand held high in the air. A hush fell over the crowd, and no one said anything for the longest time, including Bishop Abram, who appeared more stunned than anyone.

When he finally found his tongue again, he called for a higher bid, but no one made a motion to accept it. She glanced at Gabriel, who sat with his arms crossed over his chest and a scowl on his face.

"One hundred dollars! Going once, going twice...SOLD to Mr. Noah Wyse!"

Everyone clapped, and Bishop Abram held out her basket so she could come get it, but she felt glued to the seat. It took her aunt Sadie's prompting – or rather, *pushing* – to make her move, and when she retrieved the basket and turned to walk back, she didn't miss the look of contempt on Victoria Kaufmann's face.

Hope made her way to the back of the crowd and stood beside Noah as Bishop Abram picked up another basket she recognized as Victoria's. She wanted to say something to Noah, but she felt shy for some strange reason and so she stood beside him and waited for the auction to end. To say she was grateful Gabriel didn't win her basket would be an understatement, but Victoria wasn't so lucky. When he placed the highest bid on her basket, there was no denying the disapproving look on her face as she grabbed the basket from Bishop Abram's hands and sat down beside Gabriel on the front pew.

When the auction finally ended, Noah started walking in the direction of her aunt Sadie, which both intrigued and worried her as she followed him. When they approached, her aunt gave her another sly smile, but she rolled her eyes heavenward and chose to ignore it.

"Mrs. Sadie, do you mind if I take Hope home this afternoon?"

His question surprised her, but it didn't seem to faze her aunt, who agreed with more enthusiasm than she expected. When Sadie said goodbye and turned to leave, she didn't miss the little bounce in her step, and she knew without a shadow of a doubt that she would never hear the end of her aunt's gloating as soon as she returned home.

"So, where should we have our picnic?" Noah asked, after turning in his money to Bishop Abram.

Hope looked around the open space surrounding them and pointed to a large pine tree several yards away, which would help shade them from the blinding sun – and, more importantly, keep them far away from Victoria and Gabriel, who were heading in the opposite direction. Once they were settled on the blanket Hope had stowed away inside the basket, the two of them began unpacking the food.

"Noah, you really didn't have to do this. Not that I don't appreciate it, because I do, and I know the kids at the school will too when they get their new books."

Her comment made him smile.

"Oh, that reminds me, where is Ivy?" she asked.

Noah removed the aluminum foil from the plate of fried chicken and set it down between them while Hope poured two glasses of lemonade.

"She's spending the weekend with my parents. She's been begging me to stay with them for weeks now, and I finally gave in, but I didn't want to. The house is too quiet and empty when she's not there."

The tone of his voice made her heart ache, and Hope quickly changed the subject.

"I think Victoria was upset you didn't bid on her basket."

Noah chuckled. "She isn't my type. Besides, Ivy made me promise not to bid on anyone's basket except yours."

Hope almost choked on her lemonade, and she took a moment before she trusted herself to speak.

"That was very sweet of her, but I feel bad you spent so much money. I know how hard you work for it."

When he reached over and touched her hand, it felt...different. Sure, he'd accidentally brushed his hand against her skin many times over the years, but this time the warmth of his touch made her tremble, which had never happened before.

"Don't feel bad. I wanted to do it, and I had planned on doing it long before Ivy mentioned it."

Once their plates were full and Noah said grace over the food, they both started eating, and she was happy to see how much he enjoyed it, especially since she'd spent all morning cooking. They talked and laughed while they ate, and they were still sitting beneath the pine tree long after they finished their meal and the others had gathered their belongings and left for home.

Hope packed the basket and moved it out of the way as Noah stretched out on the blanket on his back and laced his fingers together over his stomach. She followed suit, being careful not to lay too close to him. The last thing she needed was for someone passing by on the main road to see them and get the wrong idea.

She sighed contentedly as she looked up at the pine tree and watched the branches sway with the wind. It was certainly a beautiful day God had blessed them with.

"Hope, can I ask you something? It's kind of personal."

She swallowed past the lump in her throat. "Of course."

When he turned over and propped his body up on his elbow so he could face her, she was suddenly very aware of how close they were. Several different emotions converged on her at once – fear, excitement, anxiety...even longing. She kept her eyes focused on the branches above her to keep from looking at him, worried that her face might betray what her mind and body were struggling with.

"Do you still not believe in love?" he asked.

Surprised by his question, Hope didn't know how to answer at first. "I've never said I didn't believe in it."

He looked at her as if she'd just made a funny comment. "Hope, come on. I know you better than anyone, and you've always made it perfectly clear that you don't want a relationship because of your parents."

She couldn't deny it, but the way he said it made her cringe. Were her feelings that transparent to everyone else she knew?

"Why does it matter so much to you what I believe?"

He sat up and rested his arms on top of his knees. He didn't answer her right away, and he avoided her gaze, but she didn't push him.

"I'm afraid your parents have poisoned your mind, and that matters to me more than you know."

Hope sat up and touched his arm, causing him to flinch in response. "Why?"

When he looked at her, there was something behind his gaze she couldn't quite grasp. Turmoil, maybe? Sadness? She didn't know, but it troubled her nonetheless. They'd had several personal conversations throughout their friendship, but this one was turning into something different...something deeper.

"When Maria died, I thought I would never be able to love again. I closed myself off to the possibility, but lately something's changed. I want that closeness in my life again. I miss it."

A twinge of jealousy caught her off guard and left her momentarily speechless. "I...I think that's wonderful, Noah. You deserve to be happy."

He solemnly shook his head as he peered ahead of him into the distance. "But the one person I feel I could have that with doesn't feel the same way, and I'm afraid there's nothing I can do to change her mind."

The way he stared at her, there was no denying who he was referring to, and the realization shocked her. She wanted to say something, but her tongue felt glued to the top of her mouth. He watched her and waited for a reaction, and all she could think of to do was run.

"We should go," she said.

Hope stood and started gathering her things, but Noah grabbed her arm to stop her. "Hope, please talk to me."

What could she say that wouldn't hurt his feelings and risk her losing his friendship? She honestly didn't know how she felt. Her heart and mind were jumbled with a thousand different emotions and none of them made sense. All she knew for certain was that she wanted to leave.

When Hope pulled free of his grasp and picked up her picnic basket, he hurriedly wadded up the blanket and followed her.

* * * *

Neither of them spoke on the ride to her house, but when Noah pulled up on the reins and brought the horse and wagon to a stop in her driveway, he quickly put his arms around her waist to keep her still before she tried to get away from him.

"Noah, please..." she whispered.

He felt her body tremble, and he wasn't sure if it was from the chill in the air or his touch, but he hoped with his whole heart it was the latter.

"No," he replied. "Not until you hear me out."

His heartrate escalated as the heat from her body sent an electric current coursing through his veins. She nodded in agreement, and he knew he should let her go, but it took every ounce of strength in him to release her.

"If it's your aunt and uncle you're worried about. I've already talked to them both, and they were very happy when I asked them if I could court you."

Hope's jaw slacked, and he instantly regretted not approaching the conversation in a gentler manner.

"You *what*?" she asked, her eyes wide and expressive.

Noah put a hand up to stop her before she flew into a tirade. "I promise I wasn't trying to do anything sneaky behind your back, but I'm determined to make you see that this...*us*...would work. You've just got to have a little faith in love, Hope. Your parents might be unhappy, but that doesn't mean you're destined to be unhappy too. I would never do anything to hurt you. You should already know that about me."

She appeared to be on the verge of crying, and he felt like kicking himself. Nothing was going as he planned, but he couldn't stop now. If he didn't get his point across before it was too late, he knew he risked losing her forever – even as a friend.

Noah gently touched her cheek and let his fingertips slide over her jaw to her lips. "I'm going to kiss you now," he murmured, softly. "Afterwards, if you can honestly tell me you felt nothing at all, then I promise I will let this go, and we'll never speak of it again."

Her eyes widened and she looked terrified, but he noticed she didn't shy away from his touch or try to stop him either. "Noah, no...I've never..."

He smiled as he tenderly cradled her head in his hands, "I know. You've just got to trust me."

When he leaned in close and pressed his lips against her own, he could tell right away how nervous she was by the way her lips quivered, but the effect she had on him was undeniable. His body burned hot with desire, and he felt the insatiable urge to take her in his arms, but he also didn't want to frighten her.

They separated for a moment, but he didn't let go. When she opened her eyes, he hoped he wasn't imagining things and that there was in fact a glimmer of want in her gaze. He didn't have to wonder long as she clutched the front of his shirt and pulled him to her. This time when their lips met there was no hesitation. She kissed him with a longing he hadn't felt in a very long time, and as their kiss deepened, she moaned softly into his mouth and gripped him tighter. When they managed to let go, they were both breathless.

"Does this mean you'll give us a chance?" he asked.

She didn't answer him right away, which worried him, but then he caught her smiling and his fears vanished. "It means I want to take this one day at a time. No rushing. If that's okay with you."

He nodded in agreement, and when she laid her head on his shoulder, he felt a renewed sense of hope that had been lost for many years. God was finally filling in the missing pieces of his life, and he looked forward to what He might have in store for him and Hope...and Ivy too.

Noah pulled her into his embrace and kissed her forehead.

"If you're by my side, that's all that matters to me," he replied.

And it was the truth. As long as they were together, everything seemed possible. Together they could face anything – and he was more than ready for the journey.

AMISH DAWN

AMANDA REESE

131

Chapter 1: Times Like This

Dawn Wittmer always thought of herself as a simple girl, and was a simple girl in the eyes of everyone, except her parents. Everything that Dawn did was wrong. How could it be that such a simple girl was never good at doing anything? Dawn knew that her parents were quite strict, but still, she wondered why she never earned their satisfaction. Her parents' disapproval came out in ways that she preferred not to consider, such as her poor self-esteem. Even when she was selling the family's produce in the market she found herself stressed and worried that she would do something wrong, give incorrect change, or lose customers by not providing the service and prices that the customers wanted.

Dawn knew so little about life; sometimes she wanted her world to be just at least a little bit bigger than the world that her parents imagined for her. Dawn would have loved to have permission to just be a little bit, well, "normal." Some of her other Amish friends had permission to go out of the house, have English friends, and even on a rare occasion have a beer or a glass of wine. She didn't want to leave the Amish community but recently the way her parents had been treating her like she was a 7-year-old again was making her go crazy and feel more anxious.

Dawn wasn't seven years old and she knew that very well. She was 18 years old and graduating school this year. She'd learned more from studying on her own than she gained from attending school in the one room schoolhouse that her parents insisted she attend. Dawn dreamed of attending university, of becoming a nurse, and helping those who were sick. She didn't agree with everything that the Amish believed, such as their views regarding medicine and the use of it. Why shouldn't those who are very sick utilize medicine if they have the chance to make use of modern medicine that could save their lives? Why did her parents have to see everything in "black and white?" Everything was always good or bad. In other words, everything was Amish or English and if it was English that meant it was not acceptable.

If her parents knew about her views on medicine or that sometimes she drank wine with her friends they would be so angry that she probably could not stay in their home. What was so terrible about having a glass of wine? She wanted to know. The smell of a nice glass of Merlot or Cabernet Sauvignon would make her evening. Just that little feeling that lifted her mood ever so slightly. She could feel the stress melt away from her heart, her head, her soul, her body with just one glass of wine. Sometime when she visited her friend Beth Troyer they would sit and play Scrabble together, passing the time, laughing, and talking. What neither her parents nor Beth's parents knew was that an English friend of Beth's would buy her wine. Sometimes she paid her friend with money if she had any, and other times with baked goods.

Beth understood Dawn. They had been friends since they were little and even though neither one wanted to consider leaving the Amish community they had some complaints with the rules. Why were there so many rules?

Chapter 2: Market Days

Dawn's life continued. Her days at the market were long. Secret Scrabble and wine nights were few and far between. Plus, it was hard for Beth to sneak the wine into her room and get it cold. There was almost no way to get the wine cold unless her English friend brought the wine already chilled and they consume it immediately.

Among the rows of sellers in the market were both English and Amish vendors. The cost of renting the space was increasing yet their sales remained more or less the same. The same customers. The weeks melted into each other, seeming almost entirely the same. She hardly had any schoolwork to do and she knew that her parents would never let her attend college. What was the point? Recently one of the other storefront owners was coming around to her store almost every day. It was almost annoying. Actually, it was annoying. Sunny Landsdale was his name. He was a fairly tall young man with wide shoulders, and his hair was pulled back in a ponytail, as if he wanted to be a girl. His name sounded much like a name for a girl too. She thought he was a little strange, but perhaps some part of him could be likeable. Dawn's thoughts drifted to her Amish upbringing. God asks us to love everyone, not just the people we like or love. Certainly, it was her job to treat everyone with respect that came to her stand, whether or not she liked her family's customers. She convinced herself to make small talk with Sunny. She even wanted to get up the nerve to ask him why he didn't cut his hair. Maybe today would be the day she would ask him.

Among the other fruit and pastry sellers, Dawn sat at her stand amid crates of tomatoes, cucumbers, onions, garlic, corn, and even carrots when Sunny approached the stand again. Perhaps more annoying than his hair was the fact that he stopped by more or less just to chat. He didn't seem to have any objective except bothering her! Was this the goal? This could hardly be the goal. Of course, it also seemed strange that he would come and buy just a single tomato or onion. He claimed that he bought fresh ingredients every day to cook dinner. Dawn presumed that although this could be true, he also apparently came around to her stand just to speak to her. Although many other people would consider this a compliment she preferred to do her work and be left alone. Not to mention that she had heard some interesting things about him. Some stories that she hoped were not true. She heard he had multiple lovers, all customers. She didn't want to hear anymore.

"My dearest Dawn, you are looking beautiful as always. Although I bet you would look stunning in a long, sleek, black evening gown! You are quite a beauty. What can I say?" said Sunny. "Well, you could say less. That would be a great start," replied Dawn. "Oh, my lovely, one day you will be my wife, just you see! But, in the meantime I will have to wait for you to choose to leave your Amish community and run away with me. Of course, a man cannot wait forever!" declared Sunny with enthusiasm. Dawn rolled her eyes and asked him, "So, what can I get for you today, Mr. Landsdale: a single tom..." Sunny interrupted her midsentence. "I thought we discussed that my name is Sunny. Still you prefer to refer to me as Mr. Landsdale. Mr. Landsdale is my father, thank you very much."

"As you wish, Sunny," Dawn heard herself say. She couldn't help but thinking about how silly his name and hair were. Sunny laughed and Dawn paused before posing her question. "Mr. Landsdale, ahem, I mean, Sunny, did you ever realize that, between your hair and your name, some people may think some strange things about you. I don't mean to be rude, but you can hear all kinds of gossip about a boy with a name like Sunny!" Dawn offered this observation with some courage. Sunny simply laughed, "Actually, I love my name, and yes, my hair too. You wanted to ask about my hair, I'm sure. No?" asked Sunny. "Well, yes, I hadn't quite gotten there yet," said Dawn.

"Well, to tell you the truth, since you know, I'm always honest about everything, like your good looks for example... anyway, as I was saying. My Dad always cut my hair very short when I was a kid and I hated it. When I finally got old enough to make my own decisions about my hair, I decided to stop cutting it. My whole family went crazy, but then they got used to it, and I realized I actually quite liked it. So, I kept it. Now the hair goes better with my name too! It keeps people on their toes," answered Sunny.

"You certainly are at least an interesting person," answered Dawn. Sunny smiled as a slightly extended pause in the conversation ensued. "Right, anyway, I need three green peppers for dinner tonight," said Sunny. "Sure, wow. Three, not one?" joked Dawn. "Yes, three," echoed Sunny as a goofy grin spread across his face. Sunny handed over $1.00, took his green peppers and walked away back toward his stand.

Dawn found herself watching him as he walked away and couldn't understand what or why she was watching. He was such a strange man. Dawn shook her head and continued scouring the market, hoping to make eye contact with potential customers. Business had been slower than usual this summer with no thanks to the opening of a super Wal-Mart on the south side of the city. That's what she guessed anyway. It's difficult to maintain customers and gain new ones when giant corporations can roll into town and capitalize on the local people's inability to lower prices to an unreasonable point. As Dawn grew lost in her thoughts about the super Wal-Mart and even surprisingly about herself the market day grew to a close. She carefully put away all the unsold food, locked the cabinets, and made her way home by foot.

Chapter 3: A Patient Man

Jane and Mason Wittmer, Dawn's parents, did not see positive changes in Dawn. In fact, they were ready to sit down with their daughter and discuss with her their knowledge of this Sunny boy. Jane and Mason were respected by the entire Amish community and were well-known and respected even in the marketplace. It had come to their attention that Sunny Landsdale, a known associate of the Amish Mafia was purchasing goods from their store, which in and of itself, is not a crime. They did not appreciate, however, that he was making conversation with their daughter. Parents know best, of course. Anyone even vaguely connected with Amish Mafia was not a friend of theirs.

They didn't like what they know about Sunny. They even considered removing Dawn from the market stand to keep Sunny away from her.

Jane and Mason decided that they needed to sit down with their daughter and discuss this situation that was ever so pressing on their minds. A good Amish daughter did her work, stayed away from unnecessary conversation with any English man, worked on the farm or in the market, prayed, and did her homework. Dawn could be quickly headed down the wrong path. On the evening following the day of the three green peppers, Jane and Mason decided to summon their daughter to the sitting area.

"Dawn!" Jane called up the stairs. "We need you to come downstairs for a minute." Dawn immediately knew that those words meant "we want to have a serious conversation with you." A million and one things were passing through Dawn's mind. Did they found out that she and Beth had been sneaking wine into the community and drinking sometimes? Will they forbid her to apply to college?

"Dawn. We want you to stay away from the Sunny boy," said Jane. "Any questions?" asked Mason, Dawn's father. Dawn stayed silent. "No comment at all?" inquired her mother. "Well, yes: you know it's not my fault who comes to buy food at our store. What, you want me to put out a sign that says only GOOD people buy food here! Are you crazy?" said Dawn. "Enough!" shouted Mason. "We just want you to be a little careful with Sunny. Don't make conversation. Give him what he purchases and be sure to count the change extra carefully. Okay?" said Jane.

"Sure, Mom... whatever," answered Dawn as she rolled her eyes without realizing what she was doing until it was too late. "Not whatever, do not talk to your Mom with that tone of voice, and don't let me see you roll your eyes again!" shouted Mason. "Yes, Dad. May I be excused?" "Yes, thank you Dawn," whispered Jane in a small voice.

As Dawn crept back up the winding wooden staircase to her room she considered the conversation. Although she was annoyed by the way they had accused her of engaging in conversation with Sunny, she was more relieved that they didn't know about the wine. She wasn't a drunk. She didn't need a drink. She just liked a glass of wine once in a while. That hardly made her a sinner, or evil, did it? She didn't think that made her a sinner. In the Bible, Mary asked Jesus to turn water into wine during a wedding when the couple ran out of wine to serve their guests. Dawn silently recounted the parable to herself and reminded herself that she was not a bad person. She simply had difficult, traditional Amish parents.

She continued working at the market after the confrontation with her parents. But as if he'd been warned away, Sunny was suddenly making himself scarce. She wondered where he had gone. Was he okay? She chided herself for thinking about whether or not he was okay. Why was she worried about Sunny? Sunny, his girlish name, his bleached pony tail, and cocky smile. What a silly man; no... what a silly boy. How old was he anyway? After a week of managing the store in the market and seeing no sign of Sunny, Dawn was just about ready to accept that he had found another girl to flirt with. Or, perhaps, he'd left town. Types like Sunny didn't usually stick around too long. But just then there was a tap on her shoulder. "Good afternoon, Ms. Wittmer. How are you today?" asked Sunny. "Just fine, thank you, but um... where have you been?" asked Dawn.

"Ah! So, you missed me, right? I knew it! I knew you'd miss me!" replied Sunny, a huge grin spreading across his face. "No, I didn't say that. I just said, where have you been?" retorted Dawn. "Of course, as you see it. Busy. That's all," replied Sunny. "Okay, so what can I get you today?" asked Dawn.

"Well, actually, I don't need any green peppers, but I did want to know if you'd like to accompany me for a smoothie!" invited Sunny in a bright, ironically sunny way. "You mean, um, like a date?" asked Dawn. "Yes. Or no. Whatever you would like it to be," replied Sunny. "You know, I'm not... um, I'll think about it," said Dawn. "You'll think about it. Okay: well, I can be a patient man. Let me know, let's say tomorrow, about our non-date. It's just a smoothie," Sunny pointed out diplomatically.

With that, Sunny turned and walked backed into the crowd of the market. Dawn found herself standing at the counter trying to catch her breath. Yes, for certain, Sunny had just asked her out on a date. Were her parents correct in saying to stay away from him? What if they were just wrong about him? It wouldn't be the first thing they were wrong about. She never had English friends before because her family forbid it. She was just curious enough what it would be like to go out with an English boy that she contemplated saying yes. As she closed the store for the day she found herself poised between her family's values and wanting to discover herself and the world for herself.

Chapter 4: More Than Just Coffee

The next day as Sunny approached the counter, without even thinking Dawn said, "Yes." Surprised, Sunny said, "Ok then, I'll be back at close to 4pm to meet you!" As Sunny turned to walk away, Dawn said, "Wait, make it 3pm outside the back entrance of the market." "Anything for my sunshine!" replied Sunny and laughed, since, after all, his name was sunshine, not hers. At precisely 3pm Dawn closed the store one hour earlier than usual and met him outside the market. Dawn found Sunny waiting for her there. "It's just a few blocks away," said Sunny.

As they walked Dawn realized she didn't know what to say at all. It was as if someone had glued her lips together. Sunny, recognizing the pause and potential awkwardness, started talking about himself. "Well, since you don't know a lot about me, I'll tell you the saga, if you want." "Sure," answered Dawn.

"I grew up in several different foster homes, bounced from one to another, and usually I ran away because my foster parents would beat or just use me for the government check. You know?" Sunny began his remarkable tale as if it were commonplace. "Actually, I'm sorry, I'm not understanding, because you know I'm Amish," admitted Dawn. Sunny started again, in an attempt to clarify: "When I was young, my parents died in a car accident. I was 4 years old. Just old enough to remember them and miss them. When you become an orphan, or your parents don't want you, the state tries to find a placement for you with another family in another home. But sometimes, these homes are dangerous. There aren't enough controls and regulations on who can become a foster parent." "Oh, I'm sorry. I had no idea," said Dawn. "Don't be. I'm just sharing with you my story. As soon as I turned 18 I was out of the system because I became a legal adult. I was homeless for a little while until I found a job at one of the stands here. They pay me cash under the table. No taxes or anything. Since then I've saved enough money to get a place, but I've never finished school. I want to get my GED someday, but that seems like a dream." said Sunny.

There was another pause in the conversation, but this time, perhaps it was a needed pause. "And now, how are you?" Dawn asked with genuine concern. "I'm well, just me," said Sunny. "But, why did you tell me this other story about your hair and your parents, when you don't have parents?" asked Dawn. "I wanted to impress you," Sunny confessed. "I didn't want you think I was just some orphan kid. In the beginning, I kept my hair long because my foster parents would rarely give me a haircut, let alone pay for me to get one. Sometimes they would destroy my hair when they cut it. So, finally, when I aged out of foster care, I decided nobody was going to cut my hair like that again, even me," explained Sunny.

"Well, anyway, that's me. How about those smoothies?" Sunny invited, apparently ready to change the subject. "Of course," said Dawn. As they sat together in the Tropical Smoothie Café, Dawn imagined that in some ways she had never considered before, she'd been given more opportunities in her strictly controlled life than an English man like Sunny. She wanted to tell him that her parents would freak out if they knew she had come out with him even for a smoothie, but then again, she thought it might be better if she said nothing. He probably could have guessed as much anyway. As they continued talking, Sunny moved his hand across the table and placed it on top of Dawn's hand. Dawn was startled and considered moving it. But she found that she didn't want to move it. Nobody in the Amish community would be this open with another. No one would tell someone else who wasn't in his or her family personal things. Why couldn't she trust Sunny? It was true he was two years older than she was, but two years was nothing. Plus, they were both legal adults, and hand-holding wasn't a crime.

Finally, Dawn got up the nerve to ask Sunny about the gossip at the market. "Sunny, can I ask you something?" Dawn inquired. "Sure," replied Sunny. "Is it true that you... you know... with other girls. Like am I just one of a bunch of other girls?" asked Dawn. "Oh, no... actually I just ignore the gossip at the market. One of my old foster parents owns a stall in the market so they made up stories about me to try to make me lose my job, but it didn't work," replied Sunny. "Oh, I thought... sorry," whispered Dawn. "Don't be, it's not a problem."

Just then Dawn looked at the clock on the wall and realized it was 4:20. If she didn't all but run home her parents would know something was up. Dawn jumped up and said a little louder than necessary, "Oh, I have to leave quickly... if I don't get home soon..." "It's a problem, right? Your parents I'm sure wouldn't like seeing someone like me with their daughter. Right?" interrupted Sunny. "Actually, yes I'm really sorry. Please. I have to go. I'll see you tomorrow at the market?" asked Dawn, "Yes, don't worry, just g,." replied Sunny.

Chapter 5: Learning to Fly

They knew. Before Dawn even made it inside the door, Jane and Mason were waiting for Dawn at the kitchen table. How could I be so stupid, thought Dawn. Of course, someone would have noticed that she closed the store an hour earlier. As Dawn approached her parents, her father started screaming, so loud, that even the neighbors on the opposite end of the community would hear him. She was positive.

"Dawn. You're going to your uncle's! We're sending your disobedient soul away! You need to learn respect, and the importance of NOT LYING TO YOUR FAMILY! End of discussion! You will not go back to the marketplace tomorrow. You will not see Sunny Landsdale ever again! Do you hear me?" raged Dawn's father Mason.

Dawn stood in silence in the kitchen and held back tears. Mason continued screaming. "Do you know what filth people like Sunny are? He is nothing. Nobody. He is a cheater and he hangs around with the type of people we do NOT associate with! Do you understand me? We know for a fact that he has purchased a gun from the Amish Mafia. We don't know why he has a gun or wanted a gun, but you cannot speak to him ever again. ARE WE CLEAR?" bellowed Mason

Dawn could do nothing except nod her head yes. Then she ran to her room. She wanted to find Beth and tell her everything. She wanted even more to speak to Sunny. Her parents didn't understand him. They didn't know him. And if he owns a gun, Dawn was sure that there was a reason. Sunny was a good man. They didn't know anything. Who were her parents to tell her about Sunny anyway? Dawn was overcome with outrage. They knew nothing. How could it be that her parents never saw anything in another way? They saw only things the way they wanted to see them! Nothing else!

Tomorrow she would be sent away. The worst thing was that Sunny would once again have one less person to speak to. He was on his own. But what was worse? Having no family, or a family that doesn't understand you and let you be who you want to be? Family should be the center or everything, the center of life, the center of love. Without family we are alone—unless of course you believe in God. Even with God on your side, you can feel lost and alone. There is something unique about having a human companion. Dawn longed to have her own family and her own companion. For the last year or two, she had felt part of a family that, although she knew loved they her very much, she felt the need to be separated from them. Was it selfish, she wondered? Maybe it was just a part of growing up, she thought.

Dawn found herself lost in her own thoughts about life. As we grow up we see life in a different light, sometimes for better, and sometimes for worse. We learned to see things through our own lenses. We saw things the way we wanted to see them. Sometimes that was a better choice and sometimes not. We learned that life does not happen in black and white. Life is an ever-changing revolving door. As we grow up we learn that a whole world exists outside the bubble that our parents gave us. Then the only option we have is to make our decisions and choose whether or not we want to fly.

Chapter 6: Nowhere to Run or Hide

The events that followed the day of the smoothie were a blur to both Dawn and Sunny. Sunny went to Dawn's family's stand to find it closed. He was concerned but decided not to worry too much. For certain something had come up at home. Then again, that was also what he was worried about. What happened at home? Was it because he met her outside the market? Did someone see them together?

Sunny began panicking, but not too much, because like always, he found a solution. He knew how to handle almost every possible problem. Running he was good at. Actually, it was his specialty. So was hiding. The thing about being a former foster kid is that you learn how to run and hide. He didn't want to run this time. He finally had a job, an address, a roof over his head. Sunny passed the whole week trying not to be concerned when the stand didn't open. Finally, a week later the stand opened again, but still Dawn was nowhere to be found. A woman, probably Dawn's mother, was operating their fruit and vegetable stand. He knew that asking her where Dawn was could make things worse for Dawn so he simply passed the stand slowly looking for any sign that Dawn had been there or was okay.

As he passed the woman at the stand studied him with a fierce gaze. Her eyes followed Sunny across the market and watched his every move. Very conscious of the fact that he was being watched, he ducked out of the market and cut down an alley in the opposite direction of his apartment. If this was life, he wasn't sure why he existed. Perhaps worse than being orphaned was the knowledge that his mother had been pregnant when his parents died in the car crash. He never knew what it was like to have a sister or brother, but guessed that if he had been left with a brother or sister, at least they could have been there for each other.

Meanwhile Dawn woke up on the far side of the Pennsylvania border. The sun rose over Tennessee on her Uncle Kemp's property. Uncle Kemp was a quiet stern man with rules, a wood-burning stove, and a dog. Uncle Kemp never married and most of the family thought he was slightly strange. Dawn's uncle left the Amish years ago and was rarely in contact with his family. He left the community not because he minded the simple life, but actually, because he'd had a relationship with an English girl and was banished from the house. After the relationship ended, he didn't want to be with anyone else, quite literally. He took the failed union as a sign that he was to live alone.

Nobody even knew what he did to make a living and nobody asked either. Dawn found some small comfort in her Uncle's cooking and the dog, a Yorkshire Collie with thick white and black fur. She loved nothing more than to cuddle up to him, especially when she needed to cry, which was more often than not these days. She helped her Uncle Kemp in all but silence as she learned to cut wood for the fire, maintain the property, and prepare meals for the two of them.

Her parents must have thought that sending her away to her Uncle's would make her beg to come home. Dawn was not going to beg to come home. That was not part of her plan. She would stay here as long as they made her stay. She didn't care about anything. Well, almost anything. There was the issue of Sunny. She found herself thinking about where Sunny was or if Sunny thought she left the market to avoid him, or perhaps he thought that she didn't like him. Actually, the opposite was true. She was realizing that she did like him, more than she thought she did.

Chapter 7: Connections

The difficult part of finding a missing person is that either the person does not want to be found, or is being held against their will. There were few to no clues about the whereabouts of Dawn. Due to Sunny's long history of learning how to survive, hide, and get needed information, Sunny knew that if he was patient, eventually he would find out where Dawn had disappeared to. He lurked around the market listening for any information about her whereabouts. Most of the sellers at Amish community stands were tight lipped. If they knew something, they weren't telling. Many of the regulars didn't know anything about Dawn, but sellers at neighboring stands, with whom Dawn was friendly, surely did. About two weeks had passed before Sunny had a stroke of luck. He was standing in the line of shops behind the row where Dawn's family's store was located. He overhead a conversation that he had been waiting to hear.

"...too bad about Dawn, really. She is a nice girl," said the one candle shop owner.

"I always thought those Amish people were a bit strange," replied the lady who owned the pastry stand.

"You know, I heard they took her away entirely. To Tennessee, I think. Yeah, the mother said to me that she was going to her Uncle Kemp's place to stay awhile. Who knows how long she'll be gone," answered the candle shop owner.

"If I didn't know any better, I would have thought those two were together anyway. Maybe they were an item, you know," said the pastry stand owner.

"Anyway, it's better to keep your eyes to your own business," stated the candle shop owner.

That was all Sunny needed to hear. They took her out of state to Tennessee to an Uncle Kemp's house. Not as much information as he would have liked, but it was certainly a good start. It had been two weeks already since he last saw Dawn and he wasn't going to let the smoothie date be the last one.

Sunny informed his employer he was going on a personal business trip and hoped that he would still have his job and his apartment when he returned. He just paid the rent again so for now he would be okay.

Sunny left the next morning before dawn broke. He paused thinking about how lovely dawn was and how perfectly named his friend Dawn was. He would find her. With a one-way bus ticket to

Nashville, Tennessee, a granola bar, a water bottle, a change of clothes, an extra pair of boxers, a smartphone and charger, a half-full small notebook with a pen in the spiral binding, and a paper map of Tennessee in his backpack, Sunny boarded the Greyhound. Sunny knew Greyhound buses very well. More than once he'd had to utilize a fake ID to buy a Greyhound ticket to escape a foster family. Although Sunny mused it was probably unnecessary to find Dawn as she wasn't in any real peril, he felt somewhat obligated in that it was very likely his fault they took her away.

More importantly, he'd never felt like he could actually be with anyone before, the way he felt about Dawn. Despite all his jokes and flirting, he did truly have feelings for her. The bus to Nashville took a good sixteen hours. It could have been done in a lot less time, but the bus stopped in every little town known to man. How was it possible? Every hour that passed Sunny found himself getting more anxious, a feeling which was new to him. He was used to feeling in control, even when he was completely alone.

Upon arriving in Nashville, he appreciated the reality that Dawn could still be anywhere within the state. He only had the name "Uncle Kemp" to go on. Sunny found a café with a free Wi-Fi sign, ordered a grilled ham and cheese sandwich and a coke and politely asked for the password. The waitress gave him the password and quickly walked away. For certain he smelled like Greyhound bus. That was never a good smell. He always met the strangest people with unique stories on Greyhound buses, but this time, he wasn't interested in chatting with anyone.

A few minutes later, Sunny's grilled ham and cheese arrived with his coke, a pile of Lay's potato chips, and a dill pickle. After immediately devouring the sandwich, chips, and pickles, he opened his smartphone and typed in cities in Tennessee. He made a list of the largest cities of Tennessee and did a person search for the name "Kemp." There were only 13 Kemps listed in Tennessee and one of them must be the uncle.

One by one he found phone number for 11 of the 13 Kemps. He hoped that Dawn's Uncle Kemp was not one of the 2 Kemps that didn't have a phone number.

One by one he crossed off Kemps from the list. One number belonged to a woodworking business, another to a dentist's office, another three were disconnected, and a sixth and seventh number appeared to be retirees. Sunny was feeling all but completely discouraged as he made it to the 11th number. When he dialed it, a man answered the phone and said, "Hello, Kemp here." Sunny hung up immediately. The area code proved to be in Gatlinburg. Gatlinburg it was, then. Sunny rented a room for the night, got some rest, and started off early the next morning for Gatlinburg. Another Greyhound and then a few local buses later, Sunny stepped off into Gatlinburg.

Chapter 8: Fate

While Sunny was searching the town for Dawn's uncle, Dawn herself was in despair. When would she see Sunny again? Could she return to the market? What about her dream of becoming a nurse? Was her family ever going to come back for her? Reality started to sink in that maybe her mother and father were not coming back for her. She was trapped in Gatlinburg, Tennessee. As Dawn began to panic, Sunny grew closer to finding her.

As fate would have it, finally in a local McDonald's a cashier knew the name Kemp and told him where the man lived. The worker told Sunny "Yeah, he's just a few miles away. I live in that direction and I can drop you off on the right road when my shift is over." "Thanks, that would be great. Name's Sunny, by the way," said Sunny. Two hours later Sunny was sitting in a stranger's car and growing closer to his destination.

Dawn was outside in the woods preparing a fire for the evening as the sun began to set. Her Uncle was inside, quiet as usual, preparing some sausages for the fire, when Sunny rounded the bend in the road. Dawn was startled as she recognized him, screamed, and jumped up.

Her Uncle came running, and found an equal surprise in recognizing what was transpiring. Sunny, the boy that his sister wanted to keep away from his niece, has somehow tracked her down to this unlikely location. Well, since the boy was here already, there was no sense in throwing him back into the street at night. They would of course have separate rooms on opposite sides of the house.

The three found themselves face to face in front of the fire. Uncle Kemp approached Sunny before Dawn did. "So, you must be Sunny," said Uncle Kemp. "Yessir," replied Sunny. Uncle Kemp started slowly "Well, as you can see, I'm not too keen on visitors, but since you're already here, you may as well have a sausage or two."

Dawn carefully and awkwardly wandered over to Sunny as they embraced fully—not to mention quickly, as not to upset their host and make him uncomfortable. "I assume you two understand I take no responsibility for Sunny being here. And he will not sleep in the same room as you. Meanwhile, I should notify your parents that he's here, but I don't think that will be necessary," stated Uncle Kemp.

Uncle Kemp bowed his head and went inside to give them a few moments of privacy. "How did you find me?" asked Dawn. "I'm an ex-foster kid, remember. I know how to find anyone and how to lose anyone," replied Sunny. "Right, of course," said Dawn. "Look, I don't know what to say. I like you a lot. And I don't know how I feel about being stuck here in Tennessee," continued Dawn. Sunny replied, "Well, it sounds like a pretty awful thing, but your folks do care about you, I'm sure. They just care about you in a way that doesn't make sense for you."

Dawn leaned her head on Sunny's shoulder. His body was warm, his voice was endearing, but he very much needed a shower. "Um, Sunny, let's talk after you bathe. What do you think?" asked Dawn. "Haha, of course," replied Sunny. He chuckled as Dawn asked her Uncle if Sunny could shower. While Sunny cleaned himself, Uncle

Kemp left a clean pair of jeans and a plaid button-down shirt on the sink for him to wear.

To Uncle Kemp, Sunny seemed all right. Dawn and Sunny reminded him of when he was a kid. Kids want to be able to experiment in relationships. It's hard in today's world to keep an Amish kid within the confines of being Amish. After Sunny rejoined the fire the three sat together, lost in their thoughts. What they would do? Sunny and Dawn may care for each other a lot, but they had quite the decision to make, and soon. Uncle Kemp reluctantly told them his story about how he ended up living on his own. He told them about the English girl he fell in love with when he was 18. He told them it was their decision to make.

The fire dimmed and no logs were added to the dying embers. The night was not their friend, explained Uncle Kemp. He didn't believe in staying outside without the fire. The night belongs to evil. "We go inside," he said. Uncle Kemp showed Sunny where he could sleep.

Chapter 9: Dawn

Dawn arrived in a peculiar way. The sun rose quietly, the sky lit up with yellows, blue and even a little bit of orange. When the morning came, it seemed like there was no easy decision to make. There wasn't. Dawn could try to reconnect with her family, or she could stay and start over with Sunny. It was evident that Uncle Kemp was not going to stop them from making their own decision.

"Good morning, Dawn!" chanted Sunny. Sunny started singing and dancing circles around Dawn. As she laughed he pulled her into his arms and kissed her lightly on the lips. "Would you like to come with me? We can go anywhere we want," said Sunny with great optimism.

"I don't know, Sunny. We hardly know each other. You're a good boy, a good man, but I think we both have decisions to make." Dawn was trying to be even-handed and rational. Sunny tried to meet her halfway. "Let's do this, then. Let's go home. Ask your parents' permission to date me. We'll tell them everything. If they accept, that's great. If they don't, you have to decide what life you want for yourself, Dawn. Don't let them hold you back from anything. Be who you are," implored Sunny.

By 10am the two were packed and ready to leave with Uncle Kemp's blessing. He dropped them both at the highway with their backpacks and wished them the best. Since he was a man of few words, his last sentence was only one: "Godspeed."

Dawn and Sunny both nodded and found their way back to the center of Galinburg. Soon they were at the Greyhound station once more. A few hot dogs from a food truck proved to be enough to fill their stomachs as they made their way to Nashville. In Nashville, they decided to press forward through the night on an overnight bus. The whole way Dawn and Sunny found themselves engaged in pleasant conversation. Sunny admitted that he had a gun, but it was only to defend himself. Dawn needed no more explanations, only peace, time, and patience. She fell asleep in his arms on the bus as it rolled along through the night.

They washed themselves at Sunny's house in the morning and planned to go to her parents' house the next morning at dawn, for which she was well named. Dawn knocked on the door with Sunny next to her side. The door opened and she said, "Hi Mom. This is Sunny. He is my boyfriend. If you can accept us both, we'd like to come inside."

www.ingramcontent.com/pod-product-compliance
Lightning Source LLC
Chambersburg PA
CBHW022130150726

47992CB00002B/526